GREEN WORLDS OF C. S. LEWIS: THE ECOLOGY OF ASLAN'S REALM

Green Worlds of C. S. Lewis

THE ECOLOGY OF ASLAN'S REALM

John Gatta

Illustrated by Mary Gatta

CASCADE *Books* • Eugene, Oregon

GREEN WORLDS OF C. S. LEWIS
The Ecology of Aslan's Realm

Cascade Books
An Imprint of Wipf and Stock Publishers
199 W. 8th Ave., Suite 3
Eugene, OR 97401

www.wipfandstock.com

PAPERBACK ISBN: 979-8-3852-4359-4
HARDCOVER ISBN: 979-8-3852-4360-0
EBOOK ISBN: 979-8-3852-4361-7

Cataloguing-in-Publication data:

Names: Gatta, John, author. | Illustrated by Mary Gatta.

Title: Green worlds of C. S. Lewis : the ecology of Aslan's realm / John Gatta, illustrated by Mary Gatta.

Description: Eugene, OR: Cascade Books, 2026 | Includes bibliographical references.

Identifiers: ISBN 979-8-3852-4359-4 (paperback) | ISBN 979-8-3852-4360-0 (hardcover) | ISBN 979-8-3852-4361-7 (ebook)

Subjects: LCSH: Lewis, C. S. (Clive Staples), 1898–1963—Criticism and interpretation. | Environmental protection in literature. | Narnia (Imaginary place).

Classification: PR6023.E926 Z6475 2026 (print) | PR6023.E926 (ebook)

Biblical citations are from the NRSV.

For Mary, beloved daughter and gifted teacher

Contents

A Note on Texts and Documentation, Chronology, and Further Reading

THE ORDER IN WHICH one should read the seven installments of C. S. Lewis's Chronicles of Narnia has been much debated. Some think it makes most sense to follow the order in which they were published, others the order of the overall narrative. In this book the ordering of my commentaries follows the order of publication, except in the case of *The Magician's Nephew*. Given my sense of how the "green theme" unfolds, I thought it best to treat that volume in my second chapter, right after *The Lion, The Witch and the Wardrobe*, though it was the sixth, or penultimate volume to see publication.

To avoid a needlessly intrusive form of documentation I have chosen to cite all references to the Chronicles of Narnia from the editions published by Scholastic-HarperCollins of New York, and illustrated by Pauline Baynes, between 1950 and 1956. In each case these Chronicles citations are indicated parenthetically, by page number, within the main text rather than in footnotes. But a few footnotes do accompany citations from other sources.

The seven installments of the Chronicles are listed here (as issued by Scholastic-HarperCollins in narrative rather than publication order), together with the tag reference I have attached for abbreviation to each:

1. *The Magician's Nephew (MN)*
2. *The Lion, the Witch and the Wardrobe* (*LWW*)

3. *Prince Caspian: The Return to Narnia (PC)*
4. *The Voyage of the Dawn Treader (DT)*
5. *The Silver Chair (SC)*
6. *The Horse and His Boy (HB)*
7. *The Last Battle* (*LB*)

Among the many fine biographies and critical commentaries available on Lewis, these are books I have found especially useful:

Matthew Dickerson & David O'Hara, *Narnia and the Fields of Arbol: The Environmental Vision of C. S. Lewis.*

Alan Jacobs, *The Narnian: The Life and Imagination of C. S. Lewis.*

Robert MacSwain and Michael Ward, eds., *The Cambridge Companion to C. S. Lewis.*

Alister McGrath, *C. S. Lewis: A Life.*

Peter J. Schakel, *The Way into Narnia: A Readers' Guide.*

Michael Ward, *Planet Narnia: The Seven Heavens in the Imagination of C. S. Lewis.*

Rowan Williams, *The Lion's World: A Journey into the Heart of Narnia.*

Acknowledgments

THE SUBJECT MATTER OF this book falls outside my usual research focus on earlier American literature. Yet several things drew me to undertake the project. One encouragement has been the thoughtful, long-standing engagement with C. S. Lewis's life and work I was pleased to find sustained by several residents of the small but spirited college town of Sewanee where I live. In the summer of 2024, for example, I was pleased to share in the multigenerational program titled "Narnia on the Mountain," presented over several days in my own Episcopal parish of St. Mark and St. Paul on the Mountain. So I am grateful to the organizers of that program—including Robin Bates, Jeannie Babb, and the parish's rector, the Rev. Rob Lamborn.

I am indebted to Robin Bates, Julia Gatta, and Robert MacSwain for their willingness to read the book in manuscript and suggest improvements, though I am alone responsible for the final result. I much appreciate, too, Mary Gatta's creative gift in supplying some engaging illustrations of the text.

From start to finish of the production process, I have found it a pleasure to work with Rodney Clapp and other savvy, congenial members of his editorial staff at Cascade Books.

I also wish to thank several others for having contributed, in one way or another, to the creation of this book and to my broader sense of the conjunctions among faith, literature, and creation care. That band of kindred spirits includes Julia Bates, Arnold Benz, Christopher Bryan, Margaret Bullitt-Jonas, Robin Gottfried, and fellow leaders of the Center for Deep Green Faith, BJ Heyboer, Ross Macdonald, Jennifer Michael, Henry Parsley, Brown Patterson, Jim Peters, Bran and Cindy Potter, Mary Priestley, Andrea Sanders, Ruth Wiesenberg, and Beth Wiley.

Introduction

For millions who first encountered the Narnia books or films as youngsters, these stories exercised a formative influence on their imaginations. I don't happen to have been one of those fortunate souls. It wasn't until I was well into adulthood, in fact, that I first encountered, and was quickly drawn to absorb, the peculiar appeal of Lewis's fantasy tales. That these stories began speaking to me only at a later stage of life should confirm their capacity to engage readers of all ages. What's more, in the Gospel narratives Jesus often exhorts us elders to become as inwardly unassuming and open to grace as little children. So I hope this book may prove relevant even or especially for adults who are new to Narnia.

It's clear at any rate that for decades now the magical world of C. S. Lewis's Narnia series *has* stirred the imagination of children—and of countless older readers as well. Much about the fantasy realm of Narnia plainly takes us "out of this world." That sometimes outlandish, otherworldly feature of the story contributes much, in turn, to its charm for readers.

At the same time, however, Lewis's evocation of imaginary lands casts a good deal of light on the origin, character, and destiny of *this* world, the world we inhabit on planet Earth. Significantly, the opening note of the larger narrative, in *The Lion, the Witch and the Wardrobe,* is sounded in Earthly England, and occasioned by the air raids on London during World War II. That same volume also concludes in England. Narnia thus functions as a parallel universe. It offers a novel perspective by which readers can reimagine their own ties to the created order and the Creator of all life. It presents us with an inspiring vision of how we might grasp more deeply our rootedness in God's green Earth. That vision encompasses, too, our membership in the enigmatically unseen kingdom of God. Such an expansive vision strikes me as especially welcome at this time of heightened ecological awareness and climate crisis.

What I want to do in this volume, then, is to encourage reflection on the felt experience of inhabiting an enchanted cosmos, a sense arising for Lewis from the life of Christian faith and practice that underlies the Chronicles of Narnia. The Chronicles reflect, moreover, what I take to be Lewis's heartfelt investment in an "ecotheological" spirituality, though this latter-day term could not have figured in his vocabulary at the time he was writing.

What I have elsewhere described as a "green gospel"[1] sensibility permeates Lewis's Narnian world on several planes. In these stories the breath of divine life animates all sorts of talking and other beasts, for example, often blurring the boundary between human and nonhuman creatures. In addition to familiar Earthly animals, a full array of nonhuman creatures are native to Narnia. Among these mythically derived beings we find fauns, centaurs, nymphs, unicorns, and dwarves. Trees and other vegetative life forms, too, often display a spirited agency in Lewis's fantasy world. And as we'll see in what follows, weather and climate changes likewise influenced the unfolding of this creation story.

Lewis disclosed in autobiographical statements how, despite pessimistic leanings at various stages of life, his discovery of "Joy," as he called it, began in childhood and ripened throughout his adult years. Oddly enough, what he describes as "the first beauty he ever knew"—an experience that evoked one of his first pangs of Joy—was not stirred by any sublime landscape seen at firsthand. Nor by his encounter with another person. It arose instead from his reflecting on the sight of a biscuit tin, once brought to him and adorned by his brother with moss, twigs, and flowers to represent a "toy garden or a toy forest."[2] For most persons such a crude artifact

1. Gatta, *Green Gospel.*

2. Lewis, *Surprised by Joy*, 7.

would scarcely provoke their first life-changing exposure to beauty and Joy. Yet Lewis's account of this episode strikes me as revelatory for a couple of reasons.

First, it underscores the crucial role he attributed to the faculty of human imagination. For Lewis it amounted to much more than sportive make-believing. Like the Romantic poet Samuel Taylor Coleridge before him, he understood the Imagination to be a divinely re-creative force. He esteemed it as that vital faculty of perception by which we envision the wholeness of reality, the unseen web of connections unifying the otherwise disparate elements of God's creation. As such it reflects what we might describe today as an inherently ecological cast of mind. In the Platonic terms that Lewis took to heart even before becoming a Christian, it captures a face of reality surpassing anything seen amid the facticity of our material world. Accordingly, Lewis found that "what the real garden" of his childhood in northern Ireland "had failed to do, the toy garden did." Seen in the light of his newly awakened, visionary sense of things, "It made me aware of nature . . . as something cool, dewy, fresh, exuberant." For much of his life, therefore, Lewis not only valued but effectually *inhabited* the world of imagination. "As long as I live," he insisted, "my imagination of Paradise will retain something of my brother's toy garden."[3]

A second point dramatized by the toy garden episode is Lewis's awakening to the numinous spirit infused within the natural order. The elemental patterning of green life inscribed for him on that biscuit tin made him, as he says, "aware of nature" in a way he had never grasped before. The tin's microcosmic yet holistic representation of a living world enlivened his awareness of the grander macrocosm. Eventually, too, this elevated consciousness of the green world blended with other epiphanies from the beyond that Lewis identified as Joy—that is, with an ecstatic yearning, an unforeseen touch of something unattainable.

Prior to Lewis's adult profession of belief in a Christian God, his life-story traced a long, winding course of philosophic journeying from materialistic atheism, into pantheism and fascination

3. *Surprised by Joy*, 7.

with the poetic reach of Nordic and Celtic mythologies, through to an acceptance of a generic Supreme Being not yet made flesh in Christ. But even before his fuller conversion to Christianity he seems to have interpreted his encounter with Joy as an opening toward transcendence, a glimpse of the beyond that was often, though not always, made palpable to him as a presence discernible in the green world. His sense that there really was such a thing as "Joy," or what he would later call "deeper magic," persisted through it all. And it's precisely because he so thoroughly imbued the Chronicles with this same sense, apart from explicit reference to Christian doctrine, that the work has long engaged readers of all sorts and conditions.

Undoubtedly, though, the overarching faith that inspired Lewis's Narnia tales was something other than a pagan "nature religion" as such. It was instead a heartfelt Christian vision of the Creator's all-embracing love for, and involvement with, his own creation. Lewis regarded the natural order as a medium of spirit, worthy of *reverence*, but not of the *worship* to be exercised toward God alone. He therefore rejected pantheistic notions that would virtually equate nature with nature's fountainhead in the Lord of life. For if nature is taken to be divine, pure and simple, it ceases to be sacramental. "It is surely," he insisted elsewhere, "just because the natural objects are no longer taken to be themselves Divine that they can now be magnificent symbols of Divinity" that declare God's glory. But there is "a sense in which Nature-worship silences her."[4]

Lewis denied having framed his Narnia tales as openly allegorical. He preferred to say that they derived from "supposals"—that is, his exploration of various "what if" propositions. Yet Christian imagery and values plainly underlie the series. Rowan Williams confirms that there is indeed "a strong, coherent spiritual and theological vision shaping all the stories."[5] This point is most apparent in the christological bearing of Lewis's lead character of Aslan, a wild lion who radiates numinous powers of creation,

4. Lewis, *Reflections on the Psalms,* 81–83.

5. Williams, *Lion's World,* 4.

wisdom, redemption, forgiveness, and love. As we've already observed, Lewis's fantasy country of Narnia is not an altogether alien realm but comes across as a kind of figuratively conceived, parallel universe to our own world. Now and then it is even apt to remind readers of England, Scotland, Wales, or Ireland. Like the world we already know, Narnia had once found its genesis through an outpouring of divine will and love. And like the world we know, its social order is decidedly fallen—tainted by malign spirits, human and otherwise. Its natural order is likewise shown to be disordered, groaning to become more fully what it was meant and longing to be. As portrayed in *The Lion, the Witch and the Wardrobe*, even the seasonal climate rhythms of this land are sadly, to cite Prince Hamlet, "out of joint." Toward the start of *The Lion, the Witch and the Wardrobe*, Narnia suffers under the malignant and deceitful rule of Jadis, the White Witch who has managed to enlist for her evil designs sundry creatures of this land. As Mr. Tumnus, a Faun, points out, "Even some of the trees are on her side" (*LWW*, 21).

At its genesis, however, Narnia had been suffused with the goodness of Godly creation. In *The Magician's Nephew*, the prequel to the Chronicles, Aslan's voice resounds in wild but beautiful song, as he joins with other voices to sing the land of Narnia into existence. The larger narrative's re-envisioned genesis story also underscores the goodness of many other nonhuman animals, portrayed as more nearly kindred than as radically unlike the land's human residents. "Creatures," Aslan declares to these other mortals, "I give you yourselves," and "I give to you forever this land of Narnia" (*MN*, 126, 128). Many though not all animals in Lewis's fantasy are shown to be gifted, in fact, with speech and conscious intelligence.

Though Lewis manifested a keen, lifelong appreciation of animal life, he had in earlier years expressed a distinct preference for domestic animals over wilder beasts.[6] But by 1950, when he published the first of his Narnia volumes, he had for several reasons

6. I discuss some of the probable circumstances leading to Lewis's shifting attitudes toward wild animals, with special attention to his interaction with the author and spiritual guide Evelyn Underhill, in "'Not a Tame Lion.'"

been drawn to recognize—as had the Bible's author of Job before him—the distinctive holiness of animal wildness. For as conservationist Wendell Berry would later affirm, God "is the wildest being in existence."[7] Lewis elsewhere acknowledged that this lordly lion had, in effect, simply bounded his way into the story without the author's wholly conscious design to conceive such a character. In Aslan, Lewis had imagined the exceptional case of an animal character who was at once untamed and unfettered, yet decidedly godly. As one Mr. Beaver reminds Earth's four child visitors to Narnia about Aslan's disposition, "He'll be coming and going. . . . He's wild, you know. Not like a *tame* lion." Beaver had likewise responded to child Lucy's earlier query about whether Aslan was "safe" by explaining, "Course he isn't safe. But he's good. He's the King, I tell you." Aslan is in fact "the Lord of the whole wood" (*LWW*, 182, 80, 78).

The unmistakable impression of a Christ figure in Lewis's portrayal of Aslan casts fresh light, I believe, on that which is commonly termed the mystery of the incarnation. That the eternal God entered time to become fully human is regarded, in mainstream church teaching, as a crucial element of this mystery. To what extent, though, might we consider in more cosmic terms how the Creator-God's having become a *creature* (that is, having taken on animal flesh, or *sarx*), rather than necessarily and solely a human creature, is also a noteworthy dimension of the incarnation? The church's faith statement in the Nicene Creed affirms in the first place, after all, that the Creator became incarnate and thus part of creation . . . before adding the species qualifier, "and became human." And how might such musings relate to the common perception, shared by members of many faith traditions or none, that certain signs of divine presence are indeed suffused throughout God's creation—though not in the same way, or with the same consequences, as the singular Christ-event? The contemporary notion of "deep incarnation," coined by Danish theologian Niels Gregerson, derives from our current need to address questions like these.

7. Berry, "Christianity and the Survival of Creation," 101.

In the Narnia fictions, Lewis engages these questions through the provocative and even audacious stroke of presenting us figuratively with a Christly presence who takes flesh in a nonhuman animal.[8] As we've noted, he portrays this pivotal figure of Aslan as a wild beast—untamed yet clearly benign. Throughout the larger narrative, Aslan enacts the Christ-event not only through his teaching, healing, sacrificial death, and resurrection, but also through his linkage, as the Logos or creative Word of God, with a "deeper magic from before the dawn of time" (*LWW*, 156). Breathing life into others, he also displays the creative and regenerative force of divine Spirit.

It therefore seems fair to characterize the Chronicles as at least semi-allegorical. Their theological implications can scarcely be ignored. As Robert MacSwain points out, Lewis deserves to be recognized as a seminal Anglican theologian, in fact a leading theological voice of twentieth-century Christianity, despite his lack of formal training in that discipline.[9] But MacSwain aptly defines Lewis's theological accomplishment, especially in its fictive expression, largely in imaginative and artistic terms rather than in the more usual mold of abstract, systematic reasoning. In that light I think it fitting to recognize how the faith dimension of the Chronicles finds expression not through simple one-to-one allegory, with Lewis's own fictive narrative running in direct tandem with another narrative, but in the interlaced form of stories embedded within other stories.

As a literary scholar, Lewis had a keen appreciation of how this variegated intertextuality was reflected in countless ancient and later writings. He understood how, for example, the Hebrew authors' grand story of humanity's rescue from slavery, sin, and infidelity had already been embedded within Christianity's gospel story of fall and subsequent redemption. He understood well how Greek mythological tales became entwined with Roman ones and

8. Certain lines of cultural association and precedent have been identified for this leonine linkage to Christ. Lewis's christological portrayal of Aslan nonetheless strikes me as both arresting and unprecedented in several respects.

9. MacSwain, "Introduction" to *Cambridge Companion to C. S. Lewis*, 1–12.

eventually blended for him with some of the Nordic and Celtic fables, as well as with those of later fantasy writers such as George MacDonald. Something of all these precedents became absorbed into his own storytelling in the Chronicles. Within the seven chapters of his larger tale he enfolded as well reference to humankind's *most* elemental stories—recalling, for instance, the cosmic struggle between good and evil, or celebrating the journey-quest perennially undertaken by selected children of Adam, including child members of the Pevensie family.

A wealth of illuminating commentary has already been published on the Chronicles. Even the work's "green" dimensions have thus far received thoughtful, academically framed attention from critics. I have learned much, for example, from the contextualizing background and the many interpretive insights supplied by Matthew Dickerson and David O'Hara in their volume *Narnia and the Fields of Arbol: The Environmental Vision of C. S. Lewis.*

What my book looks to do, though, is something rather different from what has already been achieved in books like *Narnia and the Fields of Arbol*. That is to help general readers open the door, through an ordered process of meditation on the Narnia texts, toward a freshly interior discovery of what it might mean for them to inhabit God's own creation. My aim, in other words, is not to offer another academic elucidation, though I have some things to say on that front, so much as to kindle an ecospiritual, reflective—even, one could say, devotional—engagement with these stories.

Toward that end I've followed the same methodical sequence of treatment in almost all of the six chapters, with the one exception of chapter 4. There I thought it made most sense to discuss three of the middle Chronicles—*The Voyage of the Dawn Treader*, *The Silver Chair*, and *The Horse and His Boy*—together as an interlinked group. But in addressing every other phase of the Chronicles, I begin the relevant chapter with an Overture to identify central themes of that installment. What follows is a *précis* of the book's action, keyed to its broader import for our apprehension of God's green gospel. Then I highlight for closer deliberation some *Pivotal*

Lines from the installment in question. This *Pivotal Lines* section will mean most to readers who are reasonably familiar with the installment's full text and might well have that text ready to hand. Others could prefer to skip ahead to the concluding commentary. The chapter ends with a record of *Concluding Thoughts*, along with some questions to advance the process of meditative inquiry.

To fasten attention on keynote phrases from the text strikes me as especially fruitful in this case. For one thing, it encourages us to savor more fully the graces of Lewis's verbal artistry. Lewis was an accomplished wordsmith, after all, even when composing children's fiction. He had tried earlier in life, unsuccessfully, to gain standing as a serious poet. Yet it's fair to say that some of his finest writing, as when he tells of Narnia's creation through song in *The Magician's Nephew*, amounts to a kind of prose poetry that invites close reading and rumination. The exercise of holding in mind and taking to heart chosen phrases also has ancient precedent, in Christian and other traditions of spirituality. It is commonly represented, for example, in the *lectio divina* practice of meditating upon the scriptural Word, but is a practice applicable to other texts as well.

Many would agree that the Chronicles of Narnia qualifies as one of those texts, with potential to deepen awareness of our spiritual kinship with the whole of Creation. And because it's a narrative that traverses the full course of temporal existence, its scope is surely broad enough to reward serious reflection. As Lewis confirms in his story's ending, intended to mark no ending at all: the Pevensie children were "now at last . . . beginning Chapter One of the Great Story which no one on earth has read: which goes on forever: in which every chapter is better than the one before" (*LB*, 211).

CHAPTER 1

Entering Narnia: *The Lion, the Witch and the Wardrobe*

For most readers, this first-published volume is the obvious entryway to the Chronicles of Narnia. And for many readers it represents the most appealing and memorable of the seven installments. From the start, it unfolds a beguiling tale that invites us to accompany four children into an otherworldly land of marvels called Narnia.

But despite its charms, the adventure dramatized in *LWW* is not just an escapist fantasy. And Narnia is far from a perfected realm. Like the Earth we know, it is instead a "fallen" land. It groans to be released from its bondage—not only morally and socially, under the White Witch's tyrannical rule, but also ecologically, given the climatic blight of its perpetual winter. The time is out of joint. The forces of dissolution hold sway at the outset. The land's inhabitants are gripped by fear, anxiety, and detachment from the rhythms of seasonal change.

Yet Aslan, the leonine King of the Wood, is already moving in the land. Preparing to challenge the evil queen's rule, he is plainly a force to be reckoned with. But the saving influence Aslan means to exercise demands as well the participation of others. Divine grace typically acts in consort with that which the Lord's creatures can contribute. That's an essential feature of the larger faith Lewis reflects throughout the Chronicles. Susan, Peter, Lucy and Edmund Pevensie must all, both individually and jointly, lend their efforts toward setting things right again in this marvelous but deformed realm.

PRÉCIS OF THE ACTION

This opening installment of the Chronicles tells of how the Pevensie children—Lucy, Edmund, Susan, and Peter—first encounter Narnia. Their adventure begins amid World War II, after they had been sent from bomb-threatened London to a house of refuge in rural England. There they are by turns ushered into another, otherworldly realm, which young Lucy first discovers when she steps into a wooden wardrobe that opens into the snowclad land of Narnia. The Pevensie children are destined to play a crucial role in the future of this land. It is a realm of wonder and enchantment, but also of strife between the evil forces of the White Queen, Jadis, and an array of steadfast creatures who seek the land's restoration and advancement of the common good. These creaturely proponents of virtue hope to enlist to their cause the saving help of Aslan, the lordly lion who serves an emperor beyond the sea. For under the tyrannical rule of Jadis, Narnia continues to suffer the suppression of flourishing green life, mortal threats to its inhabitants, and a deformed climate of perpetual winter but no Christmas.

The rule of Jadis is so cruel and repressive that she can immediately turn to stone anyone who dares oppose her. She even succeeds for a time in deflecting from goodness the behavior of an otherwise virtuous character such as the Faun, Mr. Tumnus. And she exploits the personal cravings of young Edmund Pevensie to the point of his betraying his own siblings. Only through a supreme deed of self-sacrificing love on the part of Aslan, combined with a triumph of righteous combatants in the monumental battle that follows, can Jadis and her minions be destroyed. As the queen's evil spell starts to fade Father Christmas reappears, stone statues of humans and other creatures spring back to life, verdant springtime returns at last, and the blighted land of Narnia flourishes once again. This restoration of a green *shalom* is ritually confirmed by Aslan's crowning of the Pevensie children to the four thrones of just rule in Narnia. Before the next phase of their adventuring in other lands, however, they are again swept across space and time into a resumption of their former lives on Earth.

A Few Pivotal Lines . . . With Musings on Their Meaning in the Light of Green Faith

> They were sent to the house of an old Professor who lived in the heart of the country, ten miles from the nearest railway station and two miles from the nearest post office. (3)

For Lewis this prefatory note to the children's Narnian adventures had a link to personal experience since he had himself during the war provided shelter to four evacuated schoolgirls at the Kilns, his home in Oxfordshire. And at the time of composing *LWW* he, too, was on the way to becoming an "old professor." Lewis subsequently described, in *The Magician's Nephew*, the childhood adventures in Narnia once undertaken by *LWW*'s professorial character, Digory Kirke.

Here we might ponder how the larger story begins with the children's having retreated into "the heart of the country." This fairly remote, bucolic site offers the children a large house, with lots of empty passages and recesses to explore. The settlement is also, as Peter remarks, a wonderful place to encounter birds and other wildlife. It lies near mountains, woods, a stream, and a garden.

So the aura of this place, much more engaged in the natural order than anything the children could experience in London, aptly situates them in a first layer of removal from commonplace civilization, prior to their much deeper removal into the Narnian wood. While London might well be regarded, both then and now, as the functional head and cultural center of Britain, Lewis portrays the unnamed site of the professor's house as closer to the country's "heart." In the story's larger context, this heartland's isolation from any railway station or post office counts as an asset rather than detriment. It suggests that by recovering our connection to the natural order, by distancing ourselves now and then from a frenetic and materialistic world that is, in Wordsworth's language, "too much with us," we might better glimpse whatever magical worlds lie beyond our usual sight.

> He had wonderful tales to tell of life in the forest. (15)

This description of Mr. Tumnus, the Faun, reminds us that Narnia, like our own Earth, is not only a storied land but a land peopled by storytellers. Many of Narnia's animals are gifted with intelligible speech. Some of them, too, relate stories about the land and its history that end up contributing to Lewis's larger narrative project of telling stories within stories. It is from Mr. Beaver, for example, that we hear a tale about the origin of the White Witch. He tells how she is not really human at all but the offspring of a male giant and of Adam's first wife, a jinn (genie-like, possibly demonic spirit) called Lilith.

> "Even some of the trees are on her side." (21)

This warning comes from Mr. Tumnus but also reflects something of the author's views. Lewis, like his Inkling colleague J. R. R. Tolkien, thought of the arboreal realm as far from inert. Even in our own worldly sphere, to say nothing of Lewis's Narnia or Tolkien's Middle Earth, trees deserve to be regarded as vibrantly communal—rather than static or simple—life-forms. So fantasy writing by Lewis or Tolkien often attributes to trees an almost animistic, mystical capacity.

Such tales thus anticipate present-day claims, set forth by Peter Wohlleben and others, that trees can indeed communicate with each other underground and across species in hidden, complex ways. Lewis recognized, however, that not all created beings, spirits, or unseen realities should be regarded as benign. So at least "some of the trees" support the White Witch's evil cause. They possess their own sort of freedom. And insofar as Lewis saw the natural order, too, participating somehow in the "fall" and still awaiting full redemption, he cautions against endorsing naïve views of what nature romanticism might entail. Even after the White Witch's army is defeated, for example, "for a long time there would be news of evil things lurking in the wilder parts of the forest" (183).

> "It's—it's a magic wardrobe. There's a wood inside it." (25)

Some teasing wordplay appears in this remark from Lucy. The wardrobe is not only made of wood but amazingly and effectually *contains*, from the standpoint of this story's child-visitors from England, the full expanse of another country's woodland. Much of Narnian territory is itself characterized in Lewis's tale as a "wood." Although Narnia contains a few settled areas, such as the seacoast castle and royal court at Cair Paravel, its territory is largely forested. Accordingly, "King of the wood" (79) is a title commonly attributed to Aslan in *LWW*.

The permeability of space and time is a theme enforced throughout the Chronicles, and the marvelous amplitude of space that the wardrobe's wood encloses contributes to that theme. Lewis marveled elsewhere at how, in the Christian story, "what is uncreated, eternal, came into nature, into human nature, descended into His own universe, and rose again, bringing nature up with Him."[1] In accord with a well-known medieval carol celebrating Christ's incarnation, we are also invited to reflect on the wonder by which the Creator of all things was once contained in the "little space" of Mary's womb. And that other redemptive King of the wood—and Lord of all things—once reigned, of course, from the wood of a cross.

> "A door from the world of men! I have heard of such things." (35)

Like the "wood," the "door" referenced in this remark from Queen Jadis has multiple connotations, some of which surpass her own understanding. It identifies, in simplest terms, the ordinary wardrobe door through which Lucy passes for her first and later passages to Narnia, and which she is careful to leave open behind

1. Lewis, "Grand Miracle," in *C. S. Lewis Essay Collection*, 3.

her. But in grander terms, this "door" signifies the portal or gateway to another world. In that light poets have often been drawn to ponder what lies beyond "death's door." John Donne wrote, for example, of how he expected to tune his "instrument here at the door" before passing on to "that holy room" God had prepared for him. In the biblical book of Revelation, a door marks the entrance to the heart and fullness of divine life. God is portrayed there as "standing at the door, knocking," allowing that "if you hear my voice and open the door, I will come in to you and eat with you, and you with me" (Rev 3:20).

> ". . . and you are all beasts, beasts." (46)

This outburst of exasperation, spoken by Lucy in response to the doubts about her Narnian experience voiced by her siblings, carries a touch of irony shading into sarcasm. Even children's literature can, after all, traffic in authorial irony. What's ironic here, of course, is the way we commonly use words like "beastly" to bemoan the behavior of other humans even though the actual beasts—i.e., animal characters—in Lewis's story are apt to show themselves no less virtuous and generous than the children of Adam and Eve, often surpassing them in decency. In that regard I'm reminded of how another green-spirited author, Henry Thoreau, so enjoyed living near the company of animals rather than humans at his pondside rural dwelling in Massachusetts that he affixed the ironic title of "Brute Neighbors" to the relevant chapter of his classic work, *Walden*.

> "But do you really mean, sir, . . . that there could be other worlds—all over the place, just round the corner—like that?" (50)

This query, which Peter directs toward the old professor early in the story, touches on a question that occupied Lewis throughout much of his life. For a time, especially following his tutelage under William Thompson Kirkpatrick, the "Great Knock," Lewis subscribed not only to atheism but also to what he deemed a hardheaded materialism.[2] Yet even before his conversion to Christianity, materialism held little enduring appeal for him. He was more characteristically drawn to affirm the deep reality of unseen worlds, beings, and ideas. For someone of his Platonic disposition mythology and poetic imagination were, if anything, truer to life than rational empiricism. Over time he became all the more skeptical about the reliability of Enlightenment-era skepticism.

As critic Peter J. Schakel points out, Lewis's related credence in the truth-telling potential of fairy tales and fantasy found probable support in J. R. R. Tolkien's essay "On Fairy-Stories," which Lewis in 1944 helped to edit for a volume honoring Charles Williams.[3] There Tolkien had argued that "Fantasy, the making or glimpsing of Other-worlds," was "the heart of the desire" for communion with another realm identifiable as "Faërie." The successful author of fairy stories "makes a Secondary World which your mind can enter. Inside it, what he relates is 'true': it accords with the laws of that world."

What Tolkien called "the *eucatastrophic* tale" he regarded as "the true form of fairy-tale and its highest function." In its ultimate denial of "universal final defeat," the *eucatastrophic* tale offers readers a "fleeting glimpse of Joy, Joy beyond the walls of the world, poignant as grief." It thus offers readers a "gleam or echo of *evangelium* in the real world" not unlike that embedded in "the Christian Story."

Tolkien rejected the idea that fairy-stories should be written exclusively for the benefit of juvenile readers. And I believe Lewis would have been particularly impressed by Tolkien's claims in this essay for the capacity of Faërie authors to "hold communion with other living things," to disclose "Other-worlds," and even in actuality "to assist in the effoliation of Creation."[4] Neither should the reality of "Other-worlds" be limited to planets elsewhere in intergalactic space or supernatural realms apart from planet Earth. As

2. One illuminating account of Kirkpatrick's influence on Lewis is that provided by Alister McGrath in *C. S. Lewis*, 37–43.

3. Schakel, *Way into Narnia*, 27–28.

4. Tolkien, "On Fairy Stories," in *The Tolkien Reader*, 41, 37, 68, 71, 13, 73.

Lewis knew and as contemporary science also reveals to us, much on this planet that remains invisible, or that otherwise surpasses our physical senses, remains quite real and wondrous. That greater reality includes all that lives in the forest or beneath its floor, what abides in the depths of oceanic darkness, what fills the atmosphere we breathe, and all that moves within the expanses of microscopic or subatomic space. Other-worlds lie indeed "all over the place." To suppose otherwise, Lewis suggests, may well be the result of faulty education. "I wonder," mutters the professor, "what they *do* teach at these schools" (50).

> "Oh, yes! Tell us about Aslan!" said several voices at once; for once again that strange feeling—like the first signs of spring, like good news, had come over them. (78)

In the Narnian setting, the "good news" of Aslan's saving presence amounts indeed to a welcome version of "gospel" and aligns with a vernal transformation. It is telling, too, that in this story, arguably like the Christian story, recognition of his meaning and his arrival in the land comes only gradually, in discrete stages. At first we hear no word of him. Then Mr. Beaver whispers to the children a simple notice: "They say Aslan is on the move—perhaps has already landed."

And even at hearing "the name of Aslan each one of the children felt something jump in its inside'" (67–68). Then we also hear, along with the children, various stories about Aslan. Next we're alerted, through greening signs in the land and the visit of Father Christmas, that "Aslan is Nearer" (11), that his appearance is close at hand. But it is not until late in the story, in the book's twelfth chapter, that the children—and we in turn—see and hear him for the first time. That experience, we are told, is at once exhilarating and a little frightening. "People who have not been in Narnia," writes Lewis, "think that a thing cannot be good and terrible at the same time" (126). But as attentive readers we might claim to know better—that is, to have "been in Narnia" too, at least by way of imaginative involvement. And anyone who *has* been in Narnia has good reason to apprehend, Lewis suggests, the paradoxical fusion of warm familiarity with sublime wonder that Aslan's presence evokes. Surely, too, fears the children display upon their first meeting with Aslan bear the earmarks of an encounter with godliness, equivalent here to facing the *mysterium tremendum.*

> "He's the Lord of the whole wood, but not often here, you understand." (78)

It seems fitting that Aslan, in his leonine species identity, should be honored not only as monarch, but as "Lord of the whole wood." For lions happen to be recognized as the food chain's apex animal in many zoological settings on Earth. But Aslan's designation as King involves more than his brute power, his role of universal mastery. He represents instead a very different *kind* of monarch than Jadis—by virtue of his self-sacrificing disposition and overriding commitment to advancing the welfare of others. Unlike Jadis, he refuses to exercise his fullest powers, forfeiting his own capacity for omnipotence to make space for the freedom—whether directed toward good or ill—of all creatures in the land he rules. The essential conflict dramatized in *LWW* is not, therefore, the more usual clash between two contending regimes or personalities, but a moral opposition between two quite contrary conceptions of what leadership in a land should be like.

> "Wrong will be right, when Aslan comes in sight,
> At the sound of his roar, sorrows will be no more,
> When he bares his teeth, winter meets its death,
> And when he shakes his mane, we shall have spring again." (79)

These memorable lines, which the speaker Mr. Beaver identifies as an "old rhyme," fairly encapsulate the whole of Lewis's tale about a "fallen" land's salvation and restoration under grace. Significantly, this restoration, achieved mainly through Aslan's renewed presence in Narnia, is not described here as purely abstract or immaterial. It looks instead toward a blessed conjunction of moral, spiritual, and geophysical flourishing. For Aslan to "put all to rights" (79), and to trigger that great change by which "wrong will be right," is in fact comparable, in more explicitly Christian terms, to his initiating a new dawn of the kingdom of God. Aslan's coming into the land thus bears immense, life-and-death consequences. This quatrain has further biblical overtones, too, with its prophecy of a time when "sorrows will be no more" recalling Isaiah's assurance that God will in due course "wipe away the tears from all faces" (Isa 25:8). There is even a liturgical flavor to this quatrain, which apparently invites some form of chant or group recitation.

> And on the sledge sat a person, [Father Christmas], whom everyone knew the moment they set eyes on him. (106)

We might wonder whether this appearance of Father Christmas is at all warranted within Lewis's otherwise pagan, or at least outwardly non-Christian, story world of Narnia. No wonder J. R. R. Tolkien objected to its introduction here as incongruous and intrusive. We must find it startling, at any rate, to encounter amid the bleakness of the White Witch's winter this unforeseen entry of a figure beaming with jollity, clothed in a "bright red robe," and mounted on a sledge drawn by reindeer with bells. His presence is itself a great gift, and he comes laden with many other gifts, each of which is expressly suited to the needs and future role of its recipient.

Celebrating Christmas then and there seems indeed out of place at first. Seen in broader perspective, however, this interruption with its not-so-veiled reference to Christ's nativity can be read as beautifully appropriate. I take it to be dramatizing the ways in which good news of God's new creation can sometimes break in, struggling to be born, even in a pagan place and time. Grace happens, even in cultural settings beyond all knowledge of Abrahamic faiths. So perhaps it is fitting that along with chosen witnesses in the Narnian world we, too, should be startled, much as Lewis himself reports having been more than once "surprised by joy" in the course of his own life story, by the sight of Father Christmas in a place and time where he doesn't seem to belong. His appearance here, as a more affable sort of John the Baptist figure, signals in turn the greening advent of another's saving presence, whose return will restore ecological integrity to the land in accord with the story's "old rhyme" assuring us that "Wrong will be right, when Aslan comes in sight." And what the man clothed in red proclaims is "Long live the true King!"

Lewis did not, of course, invent Father Christmas. That character has a long prehistory, woven together from many strands of Christian as well as non-Christian or secular folklore, legend, and mythology drawn from many lands. No wonder this man can be identified as someone "whom everyone knew the moment they set eyes on him." He is at once St. Nicholas, Santa Claus, a partial embodiment of the Nordic Wodan or Odin, and everyone's ideal image of the bountiful gift-giver. In the biblical Letter of James (1:5), God's own self is characterized as one "who gives to all generously and ungrudgingly."

Father Christmas qualifies, too, as another embodiment of the great god Jupiter from Greco-Roman mythology, about whose relevance to *LWW* I'll be saying more toward the close of this chapter. For like Jupiter, Father Christmas serves in *LWW* as "the bringer of jollity"—to cite from the relevant tag to the fourth movement of Gustav Holtz's well-known orchestral suite, *The Planets*. In bringing to mind the jollity of Father Christmas, I like to recall the way Holtz initiates the music of his Jupiter movement with a wonderfully boisterous and buoyant flourish, before moving into the more stately, hymnlike flow of his second theme. It's mood music suited to an abrupt appearance on the scene of the enormous gift-giver. No wonder the children witnessing such an epiphany in *LWW* feel "very glad, but also solemn."

The unapologetic mishmash of Christian and pagan elements that Lewis presents in the Father Christmas episode says something important, too, about the character of Lewis's own religious faith. Having earlier, in the atheistic phase of his life, developed an imagination steeped in Nordic and other forms of mythological representation, he later came to wonder what to make of the Christian story and beliefs in the light of these competing mythologies. Must embracing Christianity displace these pagan stories, requiring the faithful to deny their truths and attraction altogether? That has historically been one perennial, rigorously "Puritan" response to the issue. Purge out all practices and beliefs which aren't demonstrably authorized by scriptural texts.

Yet that approach could never appeal to Lewis. Such age-old mythologies were actually part of what drew him toward Christian conversion in the first place. Like others before him or since, he became convinced that the gospel story of Jesus not only surpassed, but also incorporated and fulfilled the greatest aspiration of these stories. For Lewis, especially in the wake of his famous walk with Tolkien and Hugo Dyson through the grounds of Magdalen College, Oxford in 1931, the Christ story fulfilled all that had intrigued him about the old pagan myths concerning dying and reviving gods *but* with the added feature that it was a singularly "true myth," a story rooted in historical fact.[5] In countless ways the Chronicles testify to this richly layered conception of narrative, which enabled Lewis to understand how all sorts of ancient and later stories could be enfolded into his own fictive tale. The greening proclamation of Father Christmas suggests that even the fertility themes highlighted by archaic nature religions could and did, albeit with some Christianizing transformation, find a place in that larger story.

Neither did it trouble Lewis to recognize how thoroughly the archaic, Earth-inspired joy of surviving once more into the Winter Solstice, or features attributable to the Roman festival of Saturnalia, had been infused into latter-day celebrations of Christ's Nativity in December. Welcoming each year the dawn of God's new creation in Christ should, in fact, be joy enough to encompass it all. Both the Son and the Sun had indeed risen again. So for Lewis this Christian fullness of joy could and did absorb without apology all the spirits of pagan jollity, as recalled from those warmer times in Narnia "when the woods were green and old Silenus on his fat donkey would come to visit them, and sometimes Bacchus himself, and then the streams would run with wine instead of water

5. Carpenter, *Inklings*, 42–45.

and the whole forest would give itself up to jollification for weeks on end" (16).

> The trees began to come fully alive. The larches and birches were covered with green, the laburnums with gold. Soon the beech trees had put forth their delicate, transparent leaves. As the travelers walked under them the light also became green. (122)

The granular specificity and coloring of passages like this one are particularly striking. Lewis evidently knows his trees, and wants us to recognize concrete features of their variant species. With the breaking of Narnia's evil spell, the arboreal resurgence of color signals the definitive arrival of spring. And throughout the Chronicles Lewis offers us more than just a generalized homage to "nature." The spirituality set forth here is thoroughly grounded in the material world—whether that world happens to be Narnian or Earthly. In that light it is also worth noticing how Lewis throughout the Chronicles often describes, with unusual relish and particularity, what foodstuffs his characters happen to be consuming at meals.

> "Though the Witch knew the Deep Magic, there is a magic deeper still which she did not know. . . . But if she could have looked a little further back, into the stillness and the darkness before Time dawned, she would have read there a different incantation." (163)

Aslan's discourse here points out the difference between two radically distinct versions of "magic." We can take one sense of this term to describe the kind of self-serving power exercised by Queen Jadis, a force derived mainly from manipulative cleverness and secret knowledge. This capacity to apply some sort of controlling hocus-pocus squares with our usual impression of "magic." It is not nearly so powerful, or so cosmically significant, as those sacred mysteries of the faith that have no ordinary solution or

"This is no thaw," said the dwarf, suddenly stopping. "This is *Spring*."

explanation. For Lewis this "magic deeper still" than the queen's deep magic is embodied by Aslan's Christlike act of self-sacrifice, a public outpouring of love that has nothing to do with neo-Gnostic, privileged secrets of manipulation.

> "He'll be coming and going. . . . He's wild, you know. Not like a tame lion." (182)

For now it is worth reflecting, above all, on how these words highlight Aslan's identity as a figure with no fixed abode in the land. As someone who is constantly "coming and going," Aslan represents a Presence that can never be captured, controlled, or possessed. Mr. Beaver goes on to explain that "One day you'll see him and another you won't. He doesn't like being tied down—and of course he has other countries to attend to." At the close of *LWW*, it is clearly up to the other characters, especially the four Pevensie children, to sustain the godly governance and Aslanic spirit of Narnia once Aslan's physical presence has been withdrawn from this country. And we can scarcely ignore the parallel these passages suggest to the close of Jesus' bodily presence on Earth, as dramatized especially in the biblical account of his ascension and fleeting post-resurrection appearances.

> And they made good laws and kept the peace and saved good trees from being unnecessarily cut down. (183)

This excerpt from the litany of praiseworthy policies attributed to the new rule in Narnia of the Pevensie siblings sounds, from the outset, quite conventional. Most any regime practicing good governance would, one supposes, aspire to make good laws and keep the peace. These are lofty but usual civic virtues. Yet they are supplemented here by an unusually earthy, precise insistence on saving "good trees from being unnecessarily cut down." In today's context we might read about how a country's wise leaders were committed, in much broader terms, to framing and practicing "enlightened environmental policies." But it's the striking practicality of this green faith provision to *save trees*—on the part of Narnia's leaders and, by extension, from Lewis himself—that rings true.

CONCLUDING THOUGHTS

I believe that by at taking to heart simultaneously this triad of images—encompassing a domestic wardrobe, a streetlamp, and the lordly lion Aslan—we can begin to apprehend much of what Lewis's best-known Narnia volume has to tell us about green faith.

The wardrobe is, on its face, just a familiar piece of domestic furniture and a useful agent for the plot transition from Earth to Narnia. It anchors the initiation of this tale in a world the author and his readers already recognize, a point that visitors to Wheaton College, Illinois may find confirmed by an exhibit there of the actual family wardrobe once owned by Lewis. But as the portal to another world beyond Earthly reality, the wardrobe opens a way to other reflections as well. Because it is an artifact crafted from wood it calls to mind, for instance, the subtle linkage between a common feature of our built environment and the tale's primary setting in the arboreal "wood" of Narnia. Lewis repeatedly calls the Narnian environment a "wood." He tells us in *The Magician's Nephew* prequel, moreover, that this wardrobe had originally been made from an apple tree grown in London, the product in turn of a seeded core that Digory, the elder professorial character in *LWW*, had earlier brought back from Narnia. The world of Earth and of Narnia are thus interlinked.

It is likewise easy for us readers to forget that every feature we consider intrinsic to our own civilized—rather than "natural"—order of things ultimately derives from nature. In that regard Lewis inspires us to discern how the wardrobe is, in fact, a direct outgrowth of the magical yet thoroughly organic apple tree through which Digory had once found healing for his ailing mother. So yes, we're given reason to attribute special powers to this wardrobe, which stems finally from identification with that archetypal tree of life celebrated in Jewish-Christian biblical tradition as well as in pagan mythology. Representations of the tree of life can be discerned not only in the wood of Jesus' cross, but also in Scripture's opening tale of origins and its closing book of Revelation. And like his friend J. R. R. Tolkien, Lewis was intrigued by forest life and the quiet yet inspiring presence of trees.

The lamppost that Lucy notices stuck amid the snowy wood of Narnia upon her arrival there stands out initially as intrusive and radically incongruous with its setting. She stands before it puzzled, "wondering why there was a lamp-post in the middle of a wood and wondering what to do next" (9). Fair questions all. Why, after all, should a streetlamp be planted where no streets or settlements exist? Yet this Earthly artifact with its aura of the uncanny ends up offering yet another example of how certain threads of continuity lace together otherwise divergent worlds—within the Chronicles, and arguably across sundry planes of reality in the cosmos we inhabit.

For a more literal explanation of the lamppost's presence in the Narnian wood, we must again look to *The Magician's Nephew*. There we learn that it derives from the bar of a streetlamp in London that Jadis had taken back to Narnia. After she tossed it at Aslan in a fit of rage, it fell to the ground and from there grew into the lamp that Lucy is startled to find. But it lights her way, supplying both her and her siblings with an essential landmark in this trackless wood. It also defies materialistic reason—by virtue of its metallic yet magical growth from the ground like a plant, and because it glows continuously without any defined fuel source. It thus reminds us of the mostly unseen linkages, in time as well as space, that tie visible Earthly things to the reality of other worlds. Even Orual, after all, the otherwise insensitive narrator of Lewis's novel *Till We Have Faces*, is moved to wonder at times if "there might be things that are real though we can't see them."[6] Accordingly, the lamp-post marks an imaginative intersection along several planes of being—between lifeless materiality and mystical organicism, between London and Narnia, and between two worlds wherein the measures of time itself differ radically.

Unlike the lamppost, which remains fixed in place, the story's leading central character of Aslan is constantly on the move. Lewis represents Aslan as a wild yet conspicuously godly and beneficent agent of this "fallen" land's salvation.

6. Lewis, *Till We Have Faces*, 141.

The story's repeated references to him as a "wild animal" do not suggest, however, anything disordered or irrational in his behavior. In relation to others, he acts instead with evident forethought. Especially in responding with compassion to Edmund's traitorous misdeeds, he displays a carefully measured judgment. What, then, does it mean to underscore Aslan's wildness? He is portrayed as such, to begin with, by virtue of his animal force and vitality. The sense of elemental nature he epitomizes reflects that which the mystical author Evelyn Underhill had described, in her earlier correspondence with Lewis back in 1941, as "the wild beauty of God's creative action in the jungle and deep sea," and therefore as "the animal existing for God's glory and pleasure and lit by His light,"[7] rather than as existing only to satisfy human needs and desires.

Above all, Aslan's wildness signifies the way in which he, like God himself, is wholly unfettered, self-sustaining, free from bondage or obligation to any creature.

Free, too, from the need to submit to any preexisting cosmic laws, including the principle of "deep magic from the dawn of time," which the White Queen recalls has been written upon Narnia's Table of Stone. Aslan's decision to accept this covenantal agreement, thereby agreeing to surrender omnipotence and to suffer death for the sake of purging Edmund's transgression, qualifies as a wholly voluntary act of love. Releasing a magic from "*before* the dawn of time" (emphasis supplied), it transcends all forms of contractual obligation. It draws instead on the divinely deeper truth that "when a willing victim who had committed no treachery was killed in a traitor's stead, the Table would crack, and Death itself would start working backward" (163).

For some of us today Lewis's formulation seems to be marred, though, by its involvement in a suspect version of substitutionary redemption. It recalls, in other words, medieval theories of the atonement that viewed Jesus' passion on the cross as a sort of necessary compensation, rendered to God the Father or the devil,

7. Underhill, cited in *Letters of Evelyn Underhill*, 301–2.

to ransom humanity from sin and death.[8] Yet what Lewis mostly highlights through Aslan's humiliation unto death is not the lion's submission to an abstract payback requirement, so much as the purely voluntary, liberating force of his sacrificial love. And "no one has greater love than this," as the Gospel of John famously declares, than "to lay down one's life for one's friends" (15:13). So instead of investing himself through creaturely sacrifice to placate an offended deity, Aslan—like the Christ of faith, within the larger story enfolding Narnia's story—consents to become God's own supreme and salvific offering.

Neither is the salvation initiated by Aslan's presence restricted to Edmund. Lewis shows that it extends well beyond him to the full array of Narnia's inhabitants, and even to the land itself. From the start of *The Lion, the Witch and the Wardrobe*, this land had long been fixed in a degraded state of isolation and alienation. The false, corrupting sovereignty of Queen Jadis posed a formidable obstacle to restoration. Nor do the story's child wayfarers from England at first offer much promise of rescue. In fact, one of these characters, Edmund, only adds to the "fallen" moral atmosphere of Narnia when he betrays his siblings to the cause of Witch-Queen Jadis out of greed and petty sibling revenge.

In outward, environmental terms, what best epitomizes the lapsed condition of Narnia is its perpetual frigidity. For a hundred years, the White Witch had been able to arrest Narnia's seasonal cycle so that winter never ends—or, as Mr. Tumnus laments, so that it is "always winter and never Christmas" (19). Narnia suffers, in other words, from the disruptive and disordering effects of climate change. This is not, of course, change of the "global warming" sort familiar to us today. But it is an unsettling disruption of normalcy nonetheless, one that dramatizes that larger state of ecological, moral, and spiritual crisis in which, as Shakespeare's Hamlet had found, "the time is out of joint."

8. For a further critique of substitutionary theories of the atonement, together with the opposing case for "deep incarnation," see Elizabeth A. Johnston, *Creation and the Cross.*

Aslan does not, however, bring about the land's restoration single-handedly. True, his agency is indispensable in putting "all to rights" in Narnia. Yet Lewis's tale also dramatizes the need for humanity and other Narnian creatures to exercise a co-creative agency with God. In the great battle with evil, for instance, which is physically enacted in the penultimate chapter of *The Lion, the Witch and the Wardrobe*, "Peter and Edmund and all the rest of Aslan's army" (175) are all expected to join forces with Aslan to quell the White Witch's league. Signs of the new creation are already in evidence once green patches start to appear on the melting landscape. But more is required for Narnia's full restoration.

Lewis affirms most clearly humankind's cooperative role in ushering in the new order through the rituals of royal investment enacted in his closing chapter for those four children from Earth. True, the regal imagery surrounding this dénouement may not strike us as compelling or relevant in our present-day setting, especially for Americans, who dispensed with monarchy centuries ago. Why, after all, should we care to learn about the elevation to title rule in Narnia of King Peter the Magnificent, Queen Susan the Gentle, King Edmund the Just, and Queen Lucy the Valiant?

For Lewis, however, monarchy became a defining principle of *The Lion, the Witch and the Wardrobe*, linked to his faith in a divine sovereignty that assured universal meaning and goodness while defying chaos and evil. Michael Ward presents a cogent argument that Lewis, in composing his seven Narnia volumes, was inspired in each case by a particular planet—and its mythological aura—from the medieval system. Ward points out that Jupiter, with his reputation for kingship and jollity, was the planetary figure most determinative in Lewis's shaping of *The Lion, the Witch and the Wardrobe*. This identification is especially relevant in the light of Jupiter's standing as the celestial king of all the planets. Alan Jacobs even contends that what the entire Narnia series is all about, perhaps more than anything else, is the issue of "disputed sovereignty."[9]

9. Ward, *Planet Narnia;* Jacobs, "The Chronicles of Narnia," in *The Cambridge Companion to C. S. Lewis*, 274.

The crowning of Peter, Susan, Edmund, and Lucy demonstrates how Aslan, as supreme King, despite holding jurisdiction over the entire land of Faerie, has nonetheless granted humans substantial though contingent sovereignty for all decisions bearing on leadership and oversight within the land of Narnia. It is they, and by extension our own species within the contemporary world, who must be held most directly responsible for tending the Earth they inhabit. It is they who must hope to be remembered ages hence for having "made good laws and kept the peace and saved good trees from being unnecessarily cut down."

QUESTIONS FOR REFLECTION AND DISCUSSION

1. In this chapter of the Chronicles Lewis suggests that at least part of what eventually *saves* the land of Narnia from degradation, tyranny, and perpetual winter is a military victory over Jadis's forces. Yet the very idea of waging war stands in some tension with teachings of Jesus, the Prince of Peace. Ordinarily, too, warfare poses its own collateral damage not only to civilians, but to animals and the land itself. To what extent, therefore, and in what ways might you perceive Lewis's frequent portrayals of armed combat to be either consistent or inconsistent with what his story otherwise shows us about *reverence for life*?
2. *LWW* dramatizes how Aslan, through his self-sacrificing love, has effectually released Edmund, at least, from the guilt and grave penalty of his sinfulness. But do you believe, from what you can glean from the story, that Aslan's death accomplishes anything to benefit others—human or otherwise—beyond that single case of Edmund?
3. Like the biblical Jesus, Aslan clearly exercises a decisive influence upon the outcome of *LWW* through his presence, death, and resurrection. But what about his teaching? What sort of moral and spiritual instruction do you think Aslan ends up conveying in the course of this story, either through word

or example? How might we describe his manner of pastoral counsel?

4. Throughout the Chronicles, Lewis is scarcely unique in his portrayal of animal characters gifted with speech that humans can understand, since talking animals are a familiar feature of children's fiction. But the Chronicles differ from other fantasy literature in representing only some animals as capable of intelligible language, others as "dumb." What do you take to be the significance of this distinction, as well as of Lewis's broader representation of animal language?

CHAPTER 2

Narnia's Creation in *The Magician's Nephew*

WHERE DID EVERYTHING AROUND us come from? How did life itself begin? Where and when did our vast array of plants and animals, including our own species, come to be?

Such questions have long inspired the creation stories of cultures across our globe. Yet tales about "the beginning" of things commonly develop not from the start, but at some later stage of a culture's common experience and search for self-definition. That's true, for example, of ancient Israel's impulse to define its Sabbath-day celebration of creation, as reflected in chapters 1–2 of the book of Genesis. This particular segment of first-things storytelling apparently derives from a later, so-called "Priestly" source associated with the ritual cultus of the temple in Jerusalem.

It's also a feature of Lewis's late-breaking tale, embedded in *The Magician's Nephew,* about the genesis of Narnia. Given the retrospective slant of many such origin tales, I think it's all the more appropriate that this prequel to the Chronicles should have appeared well after, rather than before, the entryway text of *The Lion, the Witch and the Wardrobe.*

Lewis's origin myth in *MN* about "The Founding of Narnia" clearly parallels the biblical accounts of how our own Earth came to be. But the author's fictive retelling of the Genesis stories includes a fair measure of re-visioning. Several features set this version apart from the familiar account of Eden's emergence on Earth. In Lewis's creation tale the lordly lion, Aslan, sings rather than speaks the new world of Narnia into being. And unlike the version told in Genesis 1–2, Narnia's creation story culminates in the birth not of our own human species, but of animals gifted with intelligible speech who will become the land's central consciousness. These talking animals are also called to consent to their full emergence. And while humans from elsewhere play a noteworthy role in determining Narnia's future, they take no part in the Narnian fable of origins.

But if the *manner* of Narnia's creation differs in some respects from that operative in our own world according to Genesis 1–2, the *motive* for creation shows much consistency across the two stories. In both cases the Lord of creation engenders a world and new life not from any intrinsic necessity, but in a spirit of pure, radically expansive love, exuberance, and joy. In the larger biblical portrayal, as well as in the way Aslan touches noses with Narnia's newborn beasts, the Creator shows a personal, intimate investment in the process of creation.

In both cases, too, the newborn creatures are expected to take an active part not only in their own being and becoming, but also in promoting the health of their larger community of creation. After Aslan as singer sounds the keynote, other beings—including trees, stars, waters, horses, rabbits, moles, beavers, leopards, and sundry wild beasts—are drawn to join their voices in glorious harmony with that keynote, and with "the voice of the earth herself." It's a symphony that echoes the book of Job and other biblical texts, wherein the morning stars join with countless other forms of being, both visible and invisible, to sing God's hymn of ongoing creation.

PRÉCIS OF THE ACTION

The Magician's Nephew stands first in the Chronicles, with respect to the larger narrative sequence, but was completed last. It describes how Aslan brought about Narnia's creation and provides an explanatory backstory to *The Lion, the Witch and the Wardrobe*. The volume recalls at the outset "something that happened long ago when your grandfather was a child," and it goes on to show "how all the comings and goings between our own world and the land of Narnia first began."

Digory Kirke, the elder professor figure of *LWW*, begins this story as a boy distraught at finding himself exiled for a time in London, removed from the pleasing rural life he had previously enjoyed. While lodging there with his seemingly daft uncle, Andrew Ketterley, and his ailing mother, he is consoled to meet a new friend, Polly Plummer, with whom he explores the house's many alluring passageways. But after Uncle Andrew corners Digory and Polly in a remote room, he declares himself a magician intent upon conducting a "great experiment" that may lead to encounter with other worlds. Toward this end he exploits the children as his guinea pigs. Through a magical power infused into colored rings, he sends Polly off, without warning, to "another world." He then presses Digory to follow her there.

At the start of their other-worldly journey, Digory and Polly both find themselves tossed into a peculiar "wood between the worlds" teeming with water pools. They can almost hear the trees growing in this warm, sleep-inducing land. The liminal character of the place also pertains to its linkage, through the variegated pools, to a vast network of worlds which, in their aggregate, constitute a multiverse.

After Digory and Polly use the colored rings to seek a way out of the wood, they land in a ruined, abandoned city, once part of the vibrant land of Charn. When Digory rashly strikes a golden bell, its deafening sound rouses from enchanted torpor Jadis, the former monarch and evil Witch of Charn, who shamelessly explains how she had destroyed all life in her land, and triumphed over her sister's rival claims to leadership, by speaking "the Deplorable Word."

From Charn, Digory and Polly embark on more passages between worlds. First carried back to London in the unwelcome company of Queen Jadis, they meet Uncle Andrew there. Jadis's imperious efforts to rule this world of planet Earth set her against many in the city, leading to a noisy confrontation at the same lamp-post that will eventually be planted in Narnia. Amid the confusion Digory and Polly again seize a yellow ring to make good their escape—initially, back to the wood between the worlds, but soon thereafter to a dark, empty world-in-the-making that will become Narnia. The children are not alone, however, because Jadis had attached herself to them throughout this magical travel, together with Uncle Andrew, a London cabby, and the cabby's horse.

These visitors hear the first signs of new genesis emerging, as wordless music, out of the dark emptiness of Narnia. "A voice had begun to sing" and is soon joined in harmony by other voices. Before long the great lion Aslan, chief singer of this music of creation, comes into view. Aslan's wild voice calls into being a multitude of celestial bodies, plants, walking trees, talking beasts and dumb beasts, together with diverse "gods and goddesses of the wood." "Creatures, I give you yourselves," he declares. "And I give you myself" (127–28).

Narnia's future has been infected, however, by the presence there of Jadis, the White Witch. Because Digory's actions had allowed her to pose this threat to the newly founded land, Aslan calls on Digory to repair the damage he had wrought. He is tasked with seizing an apple from a distant garden, situated beyond the wild western border of Narnia, and returning to plant the core of this magical fruit in Narnian soil. For a good while the resulting tree would effectively counter Jadis's efforts to tyrannize and corrupt the land. Digory fulfills his assigned task—but in the process had been tempted, after encountering Jadis in the garden, to steal an apple for himself to heal his dying mother. When he acknowledges this weakness, though, Aslan graciously permits him to take another apple, meant to heal, from the new tree. Aslan also effects the transport back to England of Digory, Polly, and Uncle Andrew.

When Digory's mother eats the magical apple, it returns her to health. And after Digory plants that apple's core (together with the magic rings) in London soil, the great tree grown from it eventually becomes the material source of the wardrobe that figures so prominently in *LWW*. With the cabby and his wife now crowned to rule in Narnia, and with Jadis's malignant powers set in abeyance, the land is blessed with peace and harmony. This fortunate state of things will endure for an appreciable time—but not permanently, as the opening chapters of *LWW* will make plain.

A FEW PIVOTAL LINES . . . WITH MUSINGS ON THEIR MEANING IN THE LIGHT OF GREEN FAITH

> "And so would you [be crying] . . . if you'd lived all your life in the country and had a pony, and a river at the bottom of the garden, and then been brought to live in a beastly Hole like this." (4–5)

Although Lewis appreciated the experiences available in dense urban settings like London, he—like Digory—also retained throughout life a strong identification with greener country scenes, including those he fondly recalled from his childhood in Ireland's County Down.

> "Men like me, who possess hidden wisdom, are freed from common rules just as we are cut off from common pleasures. Ours, my boy, is a high and lonely destiny." (21)

Uncle Andrew imagines himself to be a "great scholar" (25), a powerful magician, and an astute experimental scientist. Yet he entertains delusions of grandeur that lead him to grossly exaggerate his knowledge, expertise, and accomplishments. In fact he possesses no authentic wisdom—and scant knowledge as well. He fails to understand, for example, how best to align his use of the magic rings with his own intentions. He neither discovered nor conjured through his own ingenuity the power of those rings. He instead exploited for himself a magical power already accessible through an asset inherited from his godmother—but did so contrary to her express intentions and his promise to honor them.

In sum, Andrew comes across as more of a pseudoscientist than a bona fide empiricist. His cruelty is evident from the start. Yet by the close of *MN*, his claims to recognition as some sort of heroic genius or übermensch also sound preposterous. Not coincidentally, the claims Queen Jadis makes about her own exceptional standing in the universe parallel those set forth by Andrew—and echo verbatim his contention that "ours is a high and lonely destiny."

> "The box was Atlantean; it came from the lost island of Atlantis. . . [It] contained something that had been brought from another world when our world was only just beginning." (22–23)

Uncle Andrews's remarks here and other such references underscore Lewis's imaginative confidence that other worlds do exist, beyond the locus of our own world but perhaps even (as in the case of Atlantis) within Earth's geophysical bounds. What's more, certain features of these other worlds can at times intersect with features of our own. Such occasions occur throughout the Chronicles, as at the close of *MN* when Digory's mother recovers her health by eating a magical apple transported to England from Narnia.

> "Ah, but when I looked at that dust (I took jolly good care not to touch it) and thought that every grain had once been in another world . . ." (23)

The dust referenced here strikes me as particularly evocative. It calls to mind first the dust from which God fashioned mortal humans and to which they finally return, as related in the book of Genesis. The dust referenced there is plainly drawn from Earthly soil. But from the standpoint of today's scientific cosmology, we can also reflect on another sort of dust, relevant to the genesis of stars in the universe at large. Astral formation begins with swirls of cosmic dust (i.e., grains of silicates and carbon) that gather with hydrogen and helium to create molecular clouds and, eventually, the plenitude of stars, planets, and galaxies that constitute our physical world.[1]

In that light we might not find it so fanciful to imagine, by analogy with our own estate on Earth, how "every grain" of dust in Andrew's box from Atlantis "had once been in another world." For the totality of our own bodily stuff derives from other sites, and ultimately from stardust. It is sobering to recall that every hydrogen atom in our bodies arose from the Big Bang, some 13.8 billion years ago, and thus qualifies as the product of "another world" indeed, both in time and in space.

> "No great wisdom can be reached without sacrifice." (26)

This pronouncement from Uncle Andrew sounds oracular—and, yes, carries some larger truth, as Aslan confirms through his own self-offering in *LWW*. As spoken here by Uncle Andrew, though, it has a sharply ironic impact for readers since this would-be magician acts consistently to sacrifice other creatures, never himself, toward his own ends. And in the process he neither gains nor displays any authentic wisdom.

> "The trees grew close together and were so leafy that he could get no glimpse of the sky. . . . You could almost feel the trees growing." (31–32)

The wood between the worlds—with its dislocation of ordinary time, its profusion of vegetative life but absence of animals, and its manifold pools that immerse yet leave no moisture on human visitors—is an alien place. Its network of pools seems linked to an endlessly expansive multiverse. It's a place that Lewis imagined to be peaceful yet unsettling and uncanny. He had a fertile imagination, of course, and despite limited scientific knowledge had a lifelong interest in various strains of cosmology. Today, with the benefit of observational instruments like the Kepler, Hubble, and Webb telescopes, we can begin to appreciate all the more vividly the actual, otherworldly character of worlds in deep space

1. For information relevant to these matters, I am indebted to Arnold Benz, especially as set forth in his *Astrophysics and Creation*.

beyond our own planet. We can appreciate all the better now, too, how features like black holes, and many startling anomalies in the cosmic fabric of space-time, really do exist. We are learning from astronomers that there exist places in deep space no less bizarre and startling than the wood between the worlds. That's a latter-day discovery capable of enlivening our own sense of wonder about the universe we inhabit. And it adds a further dimension of plausibility to one's reading of the Chronicles.

> "You must learn, child, that what would be wrong for you or for any of the common people is not wrong in a great Queen such as I." (68)

Like Andrew, Jadis considers herself free to ignore all moral or legal standards that others—those deemed her inferiors—are commonly expected to observe. Although she is not, strictly speaking, a human being, this trait of arrogant antinomianism has also been evidenced, all too often, in tyrannical heads of state throughout human history.

> "She even knew that I had the secret of the Deplorable Word . . . which, if spoken with the proper ceremonies, would destroy all living things except the one who spoke it." (66).

Jadis, in deploying against her own sister and subjects the obliterating force of the Deplorable Word, betrays an absence of sympathetic regard for anyone or anything beyond herself. In doing so she also violates her own involvement in the "solemn promise"—comparable, perhaps, to later US-Soviet understandings of nuclear deterrence based on mutual assured destruction—that in the impending conflict "neither side would use Magic."

At one level, we might interpret this idea of a single word capable of achieving universal annihilation as a parodic inversion of what Christians regard as God's Logos, the universally creative and sustaining Word of creation. Recall how it's through just a succession of divine words, according to the opening Priestly account from the book of Genesis, that varied features and creatures of the cosmos come to be—that is, through a simple declaration in each case to "Let there be light" and so forth. As a writer himself and a votary of mythic tales, Lewis also, needless to say, greatly appreciated the creative power of words, which perhaps gave him insight into their destructive power as well.

> In the darkness something was happening at last. A voice had begun to sing. . . . Its lower notes were deep enough to be the voice of the earth herself. (106–7)

The way Aslan sings Narnia into existence is, to my mind, the most memorable feature of *MN*. I also find it beautifully consonant with the way other imaginative writers—ranging from the authors of the book of Job, Dante, and Shakespeare to J. R. R. Tolkien, T. S. Eliot, John Muir, and Wendell Berry—have expounded upon the music of creation.

> The earth was of many colors; they were fresh, hot and vivid. They made you feel excited; until you saw the Singer himself, and then you forgot everything else.
> It was a Lion. Huge, shaggy, and bright, it stood facing the risen sun. (110)

As in *LWW*, Aslan makes a personal appearance only late in this book. Lewis prefers an extended buildup of suspense, so that Aslan's presence in *MN* is first restricted to that of an anonymous singing voice, conveying likewise the voice of creation, well before he becomes visible here in the flesh. And when he does at last appear, he is identified only as "a Lion." Mention of his name comes later still—not until the land's "wild people" respond to the Lion's charge, two chapters on, with "Hail, Aslan" (127). What further conveys a sense of Aslan's grandeur and agency in the genesis of nature is the detail of his standing to face Narnia's newly "risen sun." The passage underscores, in fact, this Lion's kinship with the Risen One who brings to life God's new creation.

> The tree which Digory had noticed was now a full-grown beech whose branches swayed gently above his head. They stood on cool, green grass, sprinkled with daisies and buttercups. (114)

Although passages like this one purport to describe botanical features that attract Digory's gaze in the new world of Narnia, its coloring and species indications mirror just as well the flourishing life of a world we already know. More than anything else, the language here conveys Lewis's long-standing, personal engagement with green growing things. That inclination had been inspired first from his childhood surroundings in Ulster, Ireland and later sustained in Oxfordshire.

> "Thus, with an unspeakable thrill, she felt quite certain that all the things were coming (as she said) out of the Lion's head." (115)

In theological terms, Polly's remark here aligns well with traditional notions of how the whole of creation was from all eternity contained in the mind of God even prior to its material expression at time's beginning.

> "I have discovered a world where everything is bursting with life and growth. . . . The commercial possibilities of this country are unbounded." (120)

Sad to say, the crassly materialistic conception of the natural order Uncle Andrew displays here is scarcely unique to his character. It has plainly been evidenced, often to devastating effect, throughout our own human history, especially in Western civilizations from the industrial era onward.

> "Narnia, Narnia, Narnia, awake. . . . Be walking trees. Be talking beasts. Be divine waters." (126)

The creatures Aslan addresses here have already come to birth but still need to awaken to a fuller, second stage of their creation. That participatory stage calls for them to respond to the gift of life with a sign of their acceptance. It is phrased in strikingly direct, penetrating language.

> "Creatures, I give you yourselves. . . . and I give you myself." (128)

Again, the sense conveyed through the rather novel phrasing of this charge is that Aslan's creatures are expected to develop an involvement and responsibility in their own creation, conceived as an ongoing process. The intimate reciprocity implicit in Aslan's charge is also apparent here, insofar as the Lion confirms his own sustained engagement in the process: "I give you myself."

> Ever since the animals had first appeared, Uncle Andrew had been shrinking further and further back into the thicket. (136)

In *MN* the varied reactions of its Earthly characters to Aslan, and to the emergent sounds and creatures of Narnia, present us with something of a moral litmus test. Uncle Andrew fails that test on several counts. Whereas Digory and the cabby, for example, are ecstatic at hearing the singing voice that first emerges from the darkness of Narnia, Andrew "was not liking the Voice" (108). Later, he even convinces himself that the song emerging from Aslan's mouth had been no song at all, "only roaring" such as an Earthly lion produces. It is scarcely surprising either that Andrew, having on Earth conducted horrid experiments on animals, shrinks from encountering the array of beasts he sees coming to life in Narnia.

> "Very well," said the Elephant. "Then, if it's a tree it wants to be planted. We must dig a hole." (144)

Even children's literature can sometimes display an ironic humor bordering on satire. Lewis's account here of Uncle Andrew's ludicrous, painfully alienated interaction with Narnia's animals is a case in point. Having shown no respect for the land's nonhuman members, and no recognition of their distinctive botanical or zoological identities, Andrew suffers here a corresponding *reductio ad absurdum* of his own creaturely identity. If he refuses to find a place in this land that honors his fellowship with nonhumans, thus acting as a human should, he might as well be planted there as a tree. That indignity seems a fitting response to his dismissive attitude.

> In Narnia the Beasts lived in great peace and joy and neither the Witch nor any other enemy came to trouble that pleasant land for many hundred years. (200)

The story thus confirms that Narnia will for some time enjoy a harmony among its creatures that images Isaiah's famous prophecy of a peaceable kingdom. This vision of a universal shalom is never to be made permanent, however—either in Narnia or on Earth. Neither can such peaceable intervals be equated with the end-time fulfillment of God's kingdom, though they may be considered a worthy sign of it. Lewis's story will go on to chronicle plenty of future troubles in its Chosen Land before that country's elegiac terminus in *The Last Battle*.

> But inside itself, in the very sap of it, the tree (so to speak) never forgot that other tree in Narnia to which it belonged. (201)

In real-world terms, one might question the anthropomorphic turn of phrase here that supposes an individual tree could somehow "forget" another tree. In recent years, though, some naturalists have shown themselves increasingly willing to consider how forest trees can and do form multiple connections beyond themselves—with trees of other species, other organisms, and mycorrhizal fungal networks below ground. Experimental evidence now confirms that even certain vegetable organisms can display in practice something resembling memory. There is evidently a kind of Earth-memory, too, recorded in the geological record of natural history. We are just beginning today, in other words, to understand all it might mean to find that the Earth itself, together with countless organisms, really is *alive*. Perceptions that anticipate that rediscovery present themselves to us from time to time, however, in works of literary imagination including the Chronicles of Narnia.

CONCLUDING THOUGHTS

Through its exploration of two important themes, *The Magician's Nephew* says much about the character and relevance of green faith—for our own world, as well as for Narnia. One such theme invites us to ponder the beginning of things, including the creation of Narnia and the cosmos, as well as the genesis of Lewis's larger narrative. It's a theme that reaches far back in time, toward origins of the Narnian realm that Digory and Polly visit—and, by extension, of the world that we inhabit. How and why, in other words, does anything exist? What role does a divine Creator play in the continuous creation of all things? And what cooperative role might creatures themselves assume in that cosmic drama?

A second green theme that *MN* brings to light is humankind's perennial and destructive urge to gain total control over the natural order. For humans to *intervene* somehow in the workings of the nonhuman world must be deemed appropriate, if not essential, for civilization to rise and develop, or to rescue ecosystems from ills our species has already inflicted. But it is quite another matter to seek such thorough *control* of Earth's life-systems, and such triumph over all nonhuman beings and processes, as to render the very notion of "nature" obsolete. And quite another matter to deprive the nonhuman order of any freedom or life of its own apart from human designs. That project, already underway in Lewis's day and well advanced in our own era of the Anthropocene, promises to leave humankind at last in totally faithless, lonely isolation from the rest of God's creation. A dismal state of things in which, as environmentalist Bill McKibben has lamented, there's effectively nothing and nobody here but us.[2] Lewis's portrayal of Uncle Andrew epitomizes the blending of misconceived science with heartless vanity that often drives such ambition. The Witch-Queen Jadis likewise displays a baleful, all-too-familiar compulsion to control everything and everyone around her.

Lewis relates his version of Narnia's creation story within several middle chapters of *MN* centered in chapter 9, "The Founding of Narnia." This narrative roughly parallels accounts in the book of Genesis while calling to mind other biblical references. It also displays a number of original features.

2. McKibben, *End of Nature*, esp. "There's nothing there except us" (89).

To begin with, Lewis's story of first things confirms that Narnia, like our own Earth and the universe we inhabit, had a distinct point of origin. It had an actual beginning and will eventually come to an end. Our world, too, is wholly bound within finite time. Whatever the agency of its creation, to perceive the universe this way as a *created* rather than eternally existent entity would not have seemed so indisputable when Lewis was writing as it does now. That the cosmos in some form had *always* existed was a contrary view entertained in fact not only by ancient philosophers, but also by bona fide astronomers within the time of Lewis's adulthood prior to emergence of the "Big Bang" theory promulgated by George LeMaître, James Hubble, and others in the 1920s. By 1943, though, Lewis could recognize that "in one respect, as many Christians have noticed, contemporary science has recently come into line with Christian doctrine, and parted company with the classical forms of materialism." For "If anything emerges clearly from modern physics, it is that nature is not everlasting."[3]

Accordingly, Lewis portrays the abysmal prelude to creation as a dark void without form or visible features, a nonplace describable as "uncommonly like Nothing" (104). And the first note of creation emerging from this vacancy is a song. That seems fitting, especially insofar as anthropologists suggest that human song probably preceded the development of speech and language. And, of course, species other than human beings also show a capacity to sing.

The sublime music first heard in Narnia issues from a single nameless, deep, and distant voice. Its "lower notes were deep enough to be the voice of the earth herself" (106). Soon this voice joins in harmony with a multitude of other, higher-pitched voices, at which point the black sky is instantaneously set ablaze with stars, large planets, and constellations. It seems to Digory "that it was the stars themselves which were singing, and that it was the First Voice, the deep one, which had made them appear and made them sing" (107). No sooner do the stars come to birth, in other words, when they are given voice. For as Lewis surely recognized and

3. Lewis, "Dogma and the Universe," in *Essay Collection*, 118.

as the psalmist had opined long ago, the whole of creation, even without benefit of human language, tells "the glory of God." In this symphony of praise "there is no speech, nor are there words." Yet from God's creaturely chorus "their voice goes out through all the earth, and their words to the end of the world" (Ps 19: 1–4).

Only thereafter does the source of Narnia's generative voice, the singer himself, appear before Digory and Lewis's readers as a huge Lion standing before Narnia's newly risen sun. And as this Lion continues to sing the land of Narnia into fullness of life, through successive stages of creation, it is only later still—two chapters later, in fact—that the Lion's proper name, Aslan (the Turkish word for "lion"), is disclosed to us. It's worth recalling that a comparable reticence about naming the divine source of being pervades the Hebrew Bible. And from the beginning, the music of Aslan's voice plainly surpasses all ordinary speech to become wild yet supernal and enchanting song. The author's poetically stirring account of this creation parallels the evocation of that primal era of our world's creation, in the biblical book of Job, "When the morning stars sang together and all the heavenly beings shouted for joy" (Job 38:7). It echoes, too, the Pythagorean notion, pervasive throughout subsequent literary traditions that Lewis knew well, of a cosmos animated by the music of the spheres. In a scholarly work he pointed out that just as medieval and Renaissance Europeans believed that "space is not dark," they supposed that "neither is it silent" if one could be morally and spiritually attuned to hear its harmonies.[4]

Lewis's portrayal of Aslan as Creator of Narnia includes a number of pointedly christological associations as well. These features coincide with New Testament statements, in Paul's epistles and the Gospel of John, concerning the eternal Christ's conjunctive role in creation together with the Father and the Holy Spirit. The prologue to John declares that through God's enfleshed Word "all things came into being" (John 1:3). Aslan enacts the Christ-event not only through his teaching, healing, sacrificial death, and

4. Lewis, *Discarded Image*, 112.

resurrection, but also through his linkage as Logos—that is, as divine Word—with a "deeper magic from before the dawn of time."

As the fleshly embodiment of Logos, Aslan speaks at the close of chapter 9 a declarative word to his new creation that advances what he had already initiated through song. It's a word that does more than generate the physical being of his creatures. As noted already, it amounts to a poetic *invocation* (that is, a calling upon) that invites a collaborative response. It's phrased as a string of elemental imperatives and active verbs, a word so clearly spoken in love that it overrides the White Witch's "Deplorable Word":

> Narnia, Narnia, Narnia, awake. Love. Think. Speak. Be walking trees. Be talking beasts. Be divine waters. (126)

As Aslan proceeds in successive stages to complete Narnia's creation, he displays other gestures, too, that recollect those attributed in biblical texts to Jesus. At one point we're told, for example, that Aslan, staring intensely at the diverse animals gathered around him, opens his mouth but not immediately to speak. Instead "he was breathing out, a long warm breath" that "seemed to sway all the beasts as the wind sways a line of trees" (125–26). That gesture, a literalized sign of inspiration, mirrors the way Christ, following his resurrection, breathes on his disciples, suggesting thereby the inspiration of God's new creation through the Holy Spirit in John 20:22.

The Gospel writers report, too, that Jesus, in the process of healing those in need, often touched their bodily members as well as eyes, ears, or the tongue. And like Jesus, Aslan develops some very earthy, tactile connections with those he has come to save and serve. As he walks among the animals, for example, he occasionally goes up to two of them, touching their noses with his.

Through such gestures Aslan creates not just new individuals or species, but new ties of community. "The pairs which he had touched instantly left their own kinds and followed him," Lewis writes, until "at last he stood still and all the creatures whom he had touched came and stood in a wide circle around him" (124).

What I find particularly striking about Aslan's approach to creation as portrayed in *MN* is its collaborative character. Narnia's creatures, in the course of their genesis as individuals and species, are never relegated to pure passivity. Aslan had instead "called up" (113) through invitatory song the valley's green grass, had "called up" even supposedly inanimate beings like the sun and stars. And immediately after bringing the beasts into being, the Lion calls on them to participate in fulfilling their own creaturely vocation. He expects them to help in completing their creation by assenting to his call. So with diverse voices, yet singular intent, all of the land's "wild people" take part in this call-and-response liturgy:

> Hail, Aslan. We hear and obey. We are awake. We love.
> We think. We speak. We know. (127)

It is also noteworthy that the reference here to "wild people" includes countless beings other than human beings. Lewis's "people" designation includes a full roster of "gods and goddesses of the wood," as well as "all the beasts and birds" who will inhabit Narnia.

Aslan underscores his cooperative understanding of the generative process by declaring to these wild people, "Creatures, I give you yourselves" (128). For more self-conscious organisms the gift of life carries co-creative responsibilities, in other words, including the need for talking beasts to cherish and deal gently with the dumb beasts. But throughout his engagement in Narnia's genesis Aslan witnesses above all to his respect for the dignity, and the freedom within limits, of everyone and all he has made.

Within the larger story this self-abnegating regard for the autonomy of others, nonhumans as well as children of Adam and Eve, emerges as antithetical to the domineering disposition shown by Uncle Andrew and the White Witch. Both Andrew and Jadis look to exercise not just influence but total mastery over the natural order. Jadis's ambition extends toward domination of the sociopolitical order, too, in every world she encounters. Both characters reflect an outlook that is not only radically anthropocentric but egocentric as well, since they value other humans only insofar as these subordinates can advance their own ends.

Particularly within the bounds of Narnia, Jadis has the supernatural or magical power to subdue most everything and everyone to her will. For a time at least she can and does exercise virtually total control over the land's life-forms and physical environment. That tyranny causes great misery. But she cannot control her own insatiable lust for domination. She cannot control the megalomania that leads her to wage war against any who would question her will. Armed with the Deplorable Word, she cannot control the impulse to obliterate Charn and, ultimately, to assure her own destruction as related at the close of *LWW*.

It is hard to ignore the relevance that this radically Earth-defying disposition bears for human culture in our own world today. When Lewis finished writing *MN* in 1954, nuclear weapons had first been used at Hiroshima and Nagasaki nine years earlier, and the first detonation of the game-changing hydrogen bomb had taken place only two years before. By 1962 Rachel Carson, in her landmark book *Silent Spring*, had affixed to the dedication page her homage to Albert Schweitzer, known among other things for championing the principle of "reverence for life." There readers encountered this withering prediction: "To Albert Schweitzer who said 'Man has lost the capacity to foresee and to forestall. He will end by destroying the earth.'" Destroying the Earth one way or another, or at least destroying life on Earth as we know it, is scarcely by now a remote prospect. Carson went on to explain in her text how the arrogant, self-destructive supposition that humans should fully *control* nature led ultimately to the folly of warring against the very Earth, with its "fabric of life," that sustains us. A misguided conception of science, having "armed itself with the most modern and terrible weapons," had ended up turning them unwittingly, she wrote, not only toward the annihilation of insects but "against the earth." She observed how the industry spawned to manufacture synthetic insecticides had been in fact "a child of the Second World War," a by-product that emerged in the course of "developing agents of chemical warfare."[5]

Shortly after that war Lewis expressed a clear cognizance "that the atomic bomb may finally and totally destroy civilization itself" and that "the lights may be put out for ever." He pointed out, though, that other definitive endings to civilization, and to the universe itself, were not only possible but inevitable. He believed we must acknowledge the existential truth that "with or without atomic bombs the whole story is going to end in NOTHING" since

5. Carson, *Silent Spring*, dedication page, 297, 16.

"the physicists hold out no hope that organic life is going to be a permanent possibility in any part of the material universe."[6]

This farthest-sighted recognition does not, however, authorize indifference toward the fate of the Earth, or toward humankind's role in its degradation. "Christianity is not wedded to an anthropocentric view of the universe as a whole," Lewis insisted, and "there are few places in literature where we are more sternly warned against making man the measure of all things than in the Book of Job."[7]

I cannot myself, in any case, read about the White Witch's launch of "the Deplorable Word" without pondering in like manner how swiftly and irreparably our planet might now fulfill Schweitzer's dire prophecy, without any long, bloody travail of armies, and aside from all other threats including climate change. It would apparently take nothing more than issuing an equivalent of the word "Go," from a superpower head of state and a handful of that leader's subordinates, to spark the holocaust of an all-out nuclear war with horrors for all life we can scarcely imagine.

Andrew's mania to control things takes the form of debased scientific inquiry enveloped in magic. He is at once a failed magician and a failed scientist.

Even Jadis rightly discerns that he can claim at best only minor-league standing as a self-styled magician. The conjuring he applies through his magic rings succeeds in drawing Digory and Polly beyond this Earth but cannot direct the course of anyone's journeying to other worlds. He mistakes the consequences of his own designation of green vs. yellow rings. The uncommon, "secret wisdom" he claims as a magician to possess is therefore no wisdom at all, but only a species of intellectual pride. The magic he practices has less to do with revealing wondrous things to an appreciative audience than with a sinister, manipulative sleight of hand heedless of the harm imposed on others. His magic thus bears no resemblance to the spiritual wisdom inherent in Aslan's "deeper magic from before the dawn of time."

6. Lewis, "On Living in an Atomic Age," in *Essay Collection*, 362.

7. Lewis, "Dogma and the Universe," in *Essay Collection*, 122.

Andrew's experimental ventures likewise belie his standing as a true scientist. He instead manifests traits consistent with the "mad scientist" trope, prominent in earlier literary works including Nathaniel Hawthorne's tale of "The Birthmark." Andrew's inquiry is inspired neither by a genuine thirst for knowledge nor by any expectation of enlarging the understanding or improving the lives of others. It amounts instead to a self-serving, materialistic kind of pseudo-religion. That outlook enables him to applaud, when he's exposed to the flourishing of Narnia's new and colorfully varied life forms, only the splendid "commercial possibilities of this country."

Nothing Andrew perceives in Narnia seems, in fact, to delight him or stir his curiosity. He lacks altogether the sense of wonder that inquiry into the natural order provokes in authentic scientists. He is instead repulsed by the sound of Aslan's glorious music from and of the Earth. He also shrinks from any encounter with Aslan's animals. "Ever since the animals had first appeared," we're told, "Uncle Andrew had been shrinking further and further back into the thicket." And we might count it no loss if Andrew were never to emerge from that thicket.

QUESTIONS FOR REFLECTION AND DISCUSSION

1. We are bound to feel disdain for Uncle Andrew's heartless experiments on animals. None of these efforts is even directed toward human betterment. Andrew has apparently failed repeatedly in his research tests with guinea pigs, some of whom "only died" while others "exploded like little bombs." Yet some forms of animal experimentation continue to be practiced in our own society. We can also discern an application to today's culture in Aslan's call, later in the story, to avoid treating dumb animals as human "slaves." To what extent, then, and in what circumstances if any, might you consider our own employment of beasts or practices of animal experimentation

to be warranted? What kinds of animals might be, or should never be, exposed to tests for the sake of human welfare?

2. The White Witch, when she speaks the "Deplorable Word," applies a weaponry fatal not just to humans and to all her enemies in Charn, but to "all living things." But why such boundless destruction? To invoke for the sake of winning her war a magic capable of annihilating every living creature in the land seems indeed like overkill. So what do you take to be Jadis's rationale for this radical solution? What larger significance might you attribute to it, both within the story's context and in relation to our own world?

3. The "wild people" who step out of the trees in the course of Narnia's creation include not only beasts well known to us on Earth, but also an array of woodland gods and goddesses together with mythical-fantasy creatures such as Fauns and Dwarfs. Such fantasy creatures are a familiar feature of children's literature. But for us as modern adult readers what relevance, if any, might they bear toward our sense of reality, or our larger vision of creaturely existence?

4. Toward the close of *MN*, Lewis's storytelling draws heavily on the Bible's pastoral imagery of Eden, including its sense of a secluded garden together with trees and fruit that assume pivotal roles in the action. Yet Lewis's tale reflects a major adaptation and transformation of the original Eden story. What do you take to be the meaning of these changes? What features of the original Eden mythology does this conclusion of *MN* retain, and for what purpose?

CHAPTER 3

Narnia Regained in *Prince Caspian*

By the conclusion of *LWW*, we may recall, the malignant regime of Queen Jadis had been overturned. Narnia's climate and natural environment had been restored to health. The creaturely inhabitants of this land, which was never meant to be "the land of men," could then live freely under the benign rule of King Peter and his siblings. So far, so good.

But this blissful harmony with the land does not last in Narnia. Neither, of course, can we ever expect it to last for long on Earth. So at the opening stage of *Prince Caspian*, some hundreds of years by Narnian reckoning after the close of *LWW*, Narnia's landscape and civil order have been blighted once more by a false and terribly destructive monarch. King Miraz is not only a power-hungry usurper who yearns to kill Prince Caspian, his own relation and proper heir to Narnia's crown. He is also a foreigner from the distant land of Telmar who intends, together with other Telmarines, to solidify his colonizing tyranny over the nonhuman animal and mythical creatures of Narnia.

King Miraz can marshal substantial military force to counter opposition to his rule. In themselves, the land's native animals, trees, and spirits who long to see Old Narnia restored have little hope of achieving this. Yet thanks to Aslan's inspiration, and the intervention of some potent allies, they do manage to recover for a good while Narnia's standing as a peaceable kingdom. The allies in question include the four Pevensie children, summoned back to Narnia by a magic horn. Prince Caspian, too, lends his support to the Narnian cause. In doing so, he transcends his own bloodline and ethnic ties to Telmar.

Lewis's story conveys the further sense that the land itself seems to remember what it once was and is still meant to be. As such, it becomes its own ground of hope for restoration. The term "palimpsest" is relevant in that regard, since it describes the way in which a given text—or, in this case, a physical landscape—can be constantly overwritten throughout time yet retains traces of its prior identity. The land of Narnia, despite the reshaping and deformation its features have suffered from Telmarines, retains memories of the experiential history that underlies its identity.

In Lewis's portrayal the trees of Narnia become a crucial expression of that identity. The music of Narnia's arboreal presence is captivating—and effective in helping to disperse the Telmarine army. Despite the fantasy aura of the Chronicles, I think there's something quite believable about the vibrancy with which these newly awakened trees in *Prince Caspian* speak, move, and intermingle with flair through the steps of country dancing.

PRÉCIS OF THE ACTION

A year later, by Earthly reckoning, after the Pevensie children had returned to England from Narnia, they visit that land once again. By Narnian reckoning, though, this new adventure takes place hundreds of years later. While waiting in a railway station before their return to school from summer holidays, the children had been pulled abruptly, by a mysterious magic, off the platform of a railroad station in England and into another world they do not recognize at first but discover to be Narnia. They eventually learn, too, that they had been summoned there by the magic horn Susan left behind.

After their long absence, the peaceable kingdom they once ruled in Old Narnia is no more. The land is blighted now by the tyranny of King Miraz, a murderous usurper who seeks to kill

Prince Caspian, his nephew and the true heir to Narnia's crown. Miraz has also exercised an oppressive, destructive rule over the native, nonhuman inhabitants of this land—its multitude of animals, trees, and woodland spirits. He belongs to the party of human Telmarines, migrants from the distant land of Telmar, who had invaded and seized control of Narnia. Prince Caspian, though he is also a Telmarine by birth, comes to side with all those who are resisting the land's foreign domination and looking to restore its just order and integrity.

These allies of Caspian and opponents of Miraz's regime include Caspian's tutor, Doctor Cornelius, the dwarves Trumpkin and Nikabrik, the talking badger Trufflehunter, and a feisty talking mouse named Reepicheep. The four Pevensie children and, of course, the great lion Aslan, must also intervene if Narnia is to be restored. Bacchus and Silenus, figures drawn from Greek mythology, likewise contribute to the cause.

At the story's close, several events lead to the surrender of Telmarine forces and Caspian's successful accession to the throne of Narnia. First Peter challenges and defeats Miraz in single combat. Inspired by Aslan, in consort with the woodland spirits, the trees are roused to active life so as to disperse the Telmarine army and send its members on the run. These malefactors must finally give up the fight when Aslan calls forth Bacchus to destroy a bridge over the Great River where they had tried to flee. The few Telmarines who then accept Aslan's offer to relocate are transported to Earth, the site of their historical origins, through a magic door. Peter, Susan, Edmund, and Lucy Pevensie all return to England, with Peter and Susan fated never to revisit Narnia.

A FEW PIVOTAL LINES . . . WITH MUSINGS ON THEIR MEANING IN THE LIGHT OF GREEN FAITH

> "This must have been an orchard long, long ago, before the place went wild and the wood grew up." (12)

Susan speaks here. The children, before realizing that they've landed near the grounds of Narnia's former castle at Cair Paravel, find themselves in a thick stretch of forest that has grown up on a seagirt island. Desperate to locate food, they are pleased to notice there an array of apple trees full of fruit to relieve their hunger. So the area had once been settled. It had once been, in fact, the scene of their own rule as monarchs.

But even before the children encounter crumbling remains of the old castle, this environment presents some ominous signs of degraded life. It is "a good deal hotter" there than in England, and nothing in those thick woods moves—"not a bird, not an insect" (10, 7). Human alteration of the land's geography has turned a former peninsula into the latter-day island. The abandoned orchard, too, suggests from the start that during the children's long absence Narnia has become something of a ruined Eden, a lost land in need of restoration. Peter recalls how Pomona, a wood-nymph familiar to ancient Romans, had cast a spell over this same orchard to bless its flourishing at the time of its planting. But Narnia as a whole had long ceased to flourish at the start of this tale.

> "I wish—I wish—O wish I could have lived in the old days. . . .When all the animals could talk, and there were nice people who lived in the streams and trees." (42)

Even as a child, Caspian displays his heartfelt attachment to the spirit of Old Narnia despite his own ethnic heritage as a colonizing Telmarine. As his tutor is later pleased to confirm, "You also, Telmarine though you are, love the Old Things" (53). And he sustains this fidelity despite his never having lived in Old Narnia. By contrast his uncle, King Miraz, has no wish to remember or to honor that former character of the land whose identity had been so markedly defined by its nonhuman inhabitants—animals along with woodland spirits. Significantly, too, Caspian's language here indicates that he does not hesitate to call these nonhumans "nice people."

> "All you have heard about the Old Narnia is true. It is not the land of Men. It is the country of Aslan, the country of the Waking Trees and Visible Naiads, of Fauns and Satyrs, of Dwarfs and Giants, of the gods and the Centaurs, of talking Beasts." (51)

Doctor Cornelius, Caspian's tutor, here assures his young charge that the stories he's heard from his former nurse and himself about Old Narnia have all been true, whereas King Miraz's self-serving denials have all been false. Miraz had insisted that "there's no such person as Aslan" and that in Narnia "there never was a time when animals could talk" (44). Yet in making these declarations he is evidently lying to Caspian, and lying to himself as well. Paradoxically, then, the recollected *stories* that Caspian embraces about a realm he has never known experientially turn out to be more reliable than the direct *testimony* about Narnia presented by his uncle. But perhaps it shouldn't surprise us that a creative writer like Lewis would be confirming in this way the inherent yet subtler veracity of storytelling.

Cornelius underscores the point that Narnia should *not* in truth be construed as "the land of Men," even if its nonhuman inhabitants concur that humans like the Pevensie children and Caspian should be assigned crucial roles in its governance. That non-anthropocentric perspective, far from prevalent in our own world, is a hallmark of the *Prince Caspian* volume.

> "Certainly it is true," said Cornelius. "Their reign was the Golden Age in Narnia and the land has never forgotten them." (54)

Cornelius verifies the stories Caspian has heard about the glorious reign of High King Peter and his siblings in Old Narnia, assuring Caspian that across time "the land" remembers them. While this reference to "the land" doubtless includes the country's inhabitants, it also suggests an impression somehow left upon the landscape itself. The notion of a palimpsest—meaning in this context that a given place is typically mutable, multilayered, constantly being overwritten and altered by the changes and chances of life—is clearly applicable here. When the children return to Narnia, they see many changes in the land, including Cair Paravel's transformation from peninsula to island. Yet this land, like countless other places on Earth, carries within itself a certain physical memory of its past.

> "But because they have quarreled with the trees they are afraid of the woods. . . . And the Kings and great men, hating the sea and the wood, partly believe these stories, and partly encourage them." (55)

Here Dr. Cornelius suggests how the antipathy Telmarines show toward both forests and the sea epitomizes their larger disengagement from the natural order. In fact the Telmarines recognize virtually no appreciation for, or kinship with, the creatures who have long been native to the very land the Telmarines presume to rule and inhabit. Accordingly, the Telmarines show themselves to be wholly unworthy of governing Narnia.

> At each conversation Caspian learned more about Old Narnia, so that thinking and dreaming about the old days, and longing that they might come back, filled nearly all his spare hours. (56)

Passages such as this reinforce the story's unusual characterization of Caspian as someone who chooses to identify personally with a land other than the one defined by his familial and ethnic origins. Although a Telmarine by birth, he wills by adoption to become a bona fide Narnian in heart and spirit. We might therefore say, borrowing language from present-day environmentalists such as poet Gary Snyder, that Caspian thus embraces the ideal of "becoming native" to the land he inhabits.[1]

Caspian's existential investment in a community, land, and familial identity other than that of his ancestral clan also has biblical precedent. In the book of Ruth, for example, the story's title character, a Moabite, famously professes loyalty not to the clan in which she was born but to the Judean community of her mother-in-law, Naomi. In the Gospels, too, Jesus repeatedly exhorts disciples to profess loyalty to the universal community of faith, above all, rather than to whatever they perceive to be their own family obligations and origins.

> "It's not Men's country (who should know that better than me?) but it's a country for a man to be King of." (70)

1. See, for example, Snyder's "Place, The Region, and the Commons," in *Gary Snyder Reader*, 194.

This telling remark from Trufflehunter the Badger complements his insistence that Caspian "is the true King" of Narnia, coming back to true Narnia. "And we beasts remember, even if Dwarfs forget, that Narnia was never right except when a son of Adam was King" (69).

It may seem curious to us that the story requires a human monarch to govern Narnia, which is said to be "not the land of men"—i.e., neither to be possessed by humans nor largely inhabited by humans. But for Lewis the mandate in question simply fulfills humankind's distinctive vocation, expressed in the book of Genesis, to "till and keep" the land as a sacred, civic duty. This duty of governance is meant to be performed not by way of an overlordship or mastery but of humble service in the manner that Caspian presumably understands.

> "Look! Look! Look!" cried Lucy. . . . "The Lion," said Lucy. "Aslan himself. Didn't you see?" (125)

In *Prince Caspian*, as in the Gospel narratives' portrayal of the post-Resurrection Jesus, the ability to recognize Aslan's presence often has more to do with the perceiver's faith than it does with bodily sense experience. In that regard the character of Lucy exemplifies the sort of faith and trust that others in the story can rarely match. This phenomenon also dramatizes, once again, Lewis's conviction that the deepest truths of existence align with what the Nicene Creed calls "things unseen," realities beyond the ordinary reach of sensory perception or empirical evidence.

> And now there was no doubt that the trees were really moving—moving in and out through one another as if in a complicated country dance. (138)

Under Aslan's inspiration, the Narnian trees awaken toward the climactic conclusion of this story. They show themselves to be not only mobile and agile, but decidedly vocal and flamboyant. They even reveal discrete, humanlike personalities, thus blurring once again the usual boundaries between human and nonhuman, between vegetative and zoological life forms. As Lewis reports, "when they looked like trees, it was like strangely human trees, and when they looked like people, it was like strangely branchy and leafy people—and all the time that queer lilting, rustling, cool merry noise" (139).

> But soon neither their cries nor the sound of weapons could be heard any more, for both were drowned in the ocean-like roar of the Awakened Trees as they plunged through the ranks of Peter's army, and then on, in pursuit of the Telmarines. (196)

Only a little earlier, Lewis's description of the awakened Narnian trees had emphasized their colorful grace, personality, and joyful spirit expressed in dance. But as need demands, they are also a force to be reckoned with. So here Lewis highlights their elemental power, determination, and decisive influence on the course of battle.

CONCLUDING THOUGHTS

With the defeat of the White Witch and her minions, Narnia at the close of *LWW* had been rescued from tyrannical rule. But this triumph is only temporary. Telmarine invaders eventually become the new, self-interested overlords of Narnia. Through force of arms, they reinstate a tyrannical order almost as oppressive as that imposed under the White Witch.

More unmistakably than in any other chapter of the Chronicles, *Prince Caspian* thus portrays a Narnian world in which human interests damaging to the land are pitted squarely against the land's own animals, plants, and woodland spirits. And the Telmarine humans in question, aside from Caspian, certainly come across as the bad guys. They reflect the most baneful colonizing impulses of arrogance, greed, deceit, and indifference toward the welfare of those they exploit and purport to govern.

Prince Caspian sets before us, in fact, the startling vision of a land in which nonhumans of diverse stripes—rather than human beings—are meant to define that land's essential purpose, citizenship, and identity. Like Old Narnia, this ideal of a Narnia regained "is not the land of Men." It is instead "the country of Aslan, the country of the Waking Trees and Visible Naiads of Fauns and Satyrs, of Dwarfs and Giants, of the gods and the Centaurs, of talking Beasts." For as Trufflehunter laments, ever "since the Humans came into the land, felling forests and defiling streams, the Dryads and Naiads have sunk into a deep sleep" (80). Yet recovering the integrity of this country for its proper constituents seems to require, among other things, open warfare between humans and nonhumans.

Caspian, Narnia's rightful ruler, is one human resident of the land who plays no part in this degradation. Though born a Telmarine, he commits his soul to the Narnian cause after absorbing the tales of Old Narnia that Doctor Cornelius, his tutor, passed along to him. The training and wisdom that Cornelius provides are crucial to Caspian's re-education. This tutor's stories bring both the inhabitants and the landscape of Narnia's Golden Age fully to life again for Caspian, almost as though he had experienced them at first hand. From Cornelius Caspian learns how he might awaken "the trees once more," and search out "wild places of the land" (53) to discover Talking Beasts and Dwarfs in hiding. And when Cornelius leads Caspian atop a rooftop tower on a moonlit night, there to offer the prince a lesson in astronomy, he encourages Caspian's vision of the created order to expand radically, opening for him a perspective far more encompassing than the narrowly acquisitive colonialism of his Telmarine heritage.

Casting his lot with the Narnians against the cause of his blood relations, Caspian becomes an exile within his own adopted land until such time as the concerted influence of Aslan, the Pevensie children, and the nonhuman creatures of Narnia enables him to prevail. In so staunchly defending the cause of Narnia's nonhuman creatures, Caspian not only rejects the primacy of family and ethnic loyalty, but also surpasses usual notions of an implacable species divide.

Yet another way in which *Prince Caspian* witnesses to green faith is through its vibrant portrayal of arboreal life. Readers are especially apt to remember the colorful dancing and vibrant music of the Narnian trees as they come to full life toward the story's close.

"When trees dance, it must be a very, very country dance indeed. . . . The first tree she looked at seemed at first glance to be not a tree at all but a huge man with a shaggy beard and great bushes of hair."

And while this portrayal is clearly figurative, as befits the fantasy genre operative here, it also points toward an actual conviction, shared by Lewis and Tolkien, that latent within our own woody world there is a larger presence and vitality, verging on consciousness, than thoroughgoing rationalists might suppose.

QUESTIONS FOR REFLECTION AND DISCUSSION

1. In *Prince Caspian*, more pointedly than elsewhere in the Chronicles, we are reminded that Narnia is not, in essence, a land of humans. It's instead meant to be, as epitomized by Old Narnia, a land belonging to other animate creatures—though human beings may suitably fill roles of governance on its behalf. Especially during this era of the Anthropocene, we Earthlings may find it hard to image such a world. But just how, in that regard, might it stir our imaginations to recall those millions of years, before the appearance of hominids, when dinosaurs and other beasts ruled the Earth or, earlier still, ages when primitive life forms alone existed here?
2. Caspian, unlike other Telmarine humans, learns to "become a native" of the Narnian land he has chosen to make his own, rather than of the land reflecting his ethnic origins. Many of us, too, feel moved to belong to countries or regions apart from the site of our birth and upbringing. Yet developing an authentic sense of place, of belonging to the land, seems all the more difficult in a country like America, where mobility and perpetual migration is so commonplace. In that cultural atmosphere, what strategies do you suppose could help persons to identify with whatever land they actually inhabit?
3. In the New Narnia of this tale, even the country's physical geography has been substantially altered under human influence. The Pevensie children are thus distraught to find places of fond memory in ruins, and a peninsula they once knew turned into an island. In our contemporary world, too, we are used to seeing around us even more radical transformations

of the landscape—and, for that matter, of the planet at large. Some human reshaping of the physical world would seem to be justified, if not in certain cases necessary. But what criteria do you suppose should be applied to projects that markedly change the land? What degree and kinds of altering the Earth do you take to be either warranted or deplorable?

4. Caspian's tutor, Cornelius, assures Caspian that despite the Telmarine initiative to destroy all traces of the Old Narnia in the new dispensation, the "land remembers" much of the country's defining stories and core identity. In our own world, too, we can sometimes discern how landscapes we have known "remember," even by way of physical impressions, previous stages of their existence. What examples or experience of this discernment can you provide?

CHAPTER 4

Before the End: Venturing beyond Narnia's Bounds

THE PRIMARY SETTING OF Lewis's Chronicles is, of course, that enchanted land called Narnia. But even volumes of the larger tale that are centered there include episodes set in other fantasy lands or back in England. In three middle books of the Chronicles, the range of other-than-Narnian countries folded into the story becomes broader still. Much of *The Silver Chair*, for example, takes place in Underland, a realm of sleeping giants situated beneath Narnia. The land of Calormen, located to the southeast of Narnia, figures prominently in *The Horse and His Boy*. And the journeying that King Caspian undertakes with Lucy, Edmund, and their cousin Eustace in *The Dawn Treader* reaches far beyond the Narnian homeland—all the way to the world's end.

This press of the narrative outward, past usual spatial boundaries, can be seen as relevant to Lewis's ecological themes. For to adopt a green vision of things is to envision more than one's fulfillment of personal salvation, more even than the flourishing of humankind. It is to look beyond those narrower concerns toward the flourishing of all created beings on our home planet. That vision calls, in fact, for a radically expansive faith—one that is cosmic in scope, and large enough to encompass everything. A quest comparable to latter-day space exploration beyond this planet and toward the stars is indeed what Lewis dramatizes, at least by figurative extension, through the seagoing journey beyond ordinary space and time that his adventurers undertake in *The Voyage of the Dawn Treader*.

Ostensibly, at least, the protagonists of this story begin their long journey for purely practical reasons. Their aim is to locate and to re-establish, if possible, personal ties with the seven lords of Narnia who had earlier been sent into distant exile by King Miraz, Caspian's corrupt and usurping uncle. They are hoping at least to hear news of what had happened to these loyal men. They are also hoping to re-incorporate into Narnian rule and law various of the far-flung lands they believe had previously benefited from the benign influence of their empire. By virtue of the authority they continue to claim over the Lone Islands, for example, they are particularly zealous to eliminate the abuse of slave trading that had arisen there.

Yet we are also led to recognize the emerging presence of speculative and existential motives for the voyage. Reepicheep, the intrepid mouse, voices those motives more openly than anyone else on board. So it's ironically the lead character who is smallest in stature who entertains the story's grandest—even, we could say, transcendent—ambitions about the meaning of their journey. Reepicheep is driven not only by a thirst for adventure, on the physical plane, but also by a spiritually grounded quest to learn what lies in the "ultimate East" beyond all frontiers of existing knowledge:

> Why should we not come to the very eastern end of the world? And what might we find there? I expect to find Aslan's own country. It is always from the east across the sea, that the great Lion comes to us. (21)

In earlier phases of this tale, Lewis sets Reepicheeps's expansive outlook and rich curiosity about the creaturely world in sharp contrast to the surly, self-absorbed temperament of the human boy Eustace Clarence Scrubb. Eustace is indeed a repellent character—carping, spoiled, ungrateful, and often spiteful toward his fellows.

He suffers from acute alienation not only from himself, and from all sense of a Creator God, but from most anything in the natural order. Lewis, in his withering account of Eustace, tells us that he "liked animals, especially beetles," but only "if they were dead and pinned on a card" (3).

Because of his materialistic and rationalistic outlook on life, Eustace is blind to the beauty and charm of the Dawn Treader as a small vessel under sail, close to nature's elements. He admires instead the latest mechanistic marvels of his own day, including "liners and motorboats and aeroplanes and submarines" (29). Neither has he any appreciation for works of artistic or literary imagination. He likes books, presumably, but only "if they were books of information and had pictures of grain elevators or of fat foreign children doing exercises in model schools" (3). It's scarcely surprising, then, to find him incredulous that the picture of a ship on windy seas, seen in Lucy's bedroom, could serve as a portal of imagination opening into another world—in this case the world of Narnia.

Yet the conversion narrative of his eventual transformation under grace becomes a central feature of the Dawn Treader's story. On Dragon Island, after Eustace slips away from his associates to avoid the threat of a work assignment, he happens upon the lair of a dying dragon and ends up sleeping there. He dreams of carrying off great wealth. Yet his adventure ends up bringing him grief rather than treasure. Because he had been "Sleeping on a dragon's hoard with greedy, dragonish thoughts in his heart, he had become a dragon himself" (91).

Eustace is horrified to find that he now possesses claws and a large, scaly, fire-breathing body. It seems a fitting punishment, though, that a human being so scornful of animal life in its diverse forms—including, of course, Reepicheep the mouse and Aslan the great lion—should himself have been turned into an animal. Only through Aslan's saving intervention, together with the painful peeling off of his multiple dragon skins and his regenerative immersion in well water, can Eustace recover his humanity. In the process, he has also begun to heal his broken relations with fellow humans, other creatures, and the world at large. Before this transformation, he could never have understood or shared the delight in creation that Lucy expresses, as she comes ashore on one of the Lone Islands, just to be able "to smell the earth and grass" (39). Others aboard the Dawn Treader, too, find their inward sense of Creation radically transformed and enlarged as they voyage eastward.

In the story's closing episodes it is once again Reepicheep, an animal rather than human character, who plays the chief role in Lewis's description of journeying toward an endpoint of space and time in the "ultimate East." When King Caspian first asserts that he will not return to Narnia but will instead proceed with the great journey so far as to "'see the World's End,'" it is the mouse who effectively claims the authority to overrule him. As Reepicheep insists,"'You are the King of Narnia. You break faith with all your subjects, and especially with Trumpkin, if you do not return'" (238–39). It is the animal mouse, too, who alone ventures far enough east, in shallow water beyond the reach of any ship, to approach Earth's edge and the brink of eternity. In fulfilling that heroic vocation he is never to return. And like some fabled Celtic adventurers of old, he makes his way toward the last by paddling his own "coracle," an undersized hide-covered vessel.

The story does not presume to show us what it might actually be like for anyone—not even Reepicheep—to *enter* that supernal land of Aslan lying beyond all current perceptions of time and space. But like Moses gazing into the promised land, Lewis's voyagers do sense finally that they're "seeing beyond the End of the World into Aslan's country" (244). What they can glimpse of this realm reveals any number of transcendent features. They find the salty ocean turned to a peculiar form of fresh water. They hear overhead "huge white birds, singing their song with human voices in a language no one knew" (218). They marvel to see submarine forests and inhabited communities, new star constellations rising in the east, and everything suffused with a golden sunlight unlike any illumination they had previously known.[1] They are also

1. The Sun, recognized in medieval cosmology as the planet Sol, is a

startled to be introduced to former stars, agents of light such as the Old Man Ramandu, who are now personified with face and voice.

Throughout this extended portrayal of "The Beginning of the End of the World" Lewis underscores the larger need to develop ways of seeing that surpass materialistic presumptions. Eustace challenges Ramandu's visionary testimony, for example, by recalling that "In our world . . . a star is a huge ball of flaming gas." Ramandu points out by way of a rejoinder, though, that "Even in your world, my son, that is not what a star is but only what it is made of" (209).

Yet before passing into the abode of all-suffusing light, characters on board the Dawn Treader must endure a terrifying episode of passing through a stretch of deep, inexplicable darkness and silence. In this chapter titled "The Island," the adventurers feel lost in more ways than one. It's as though, in present-day astronomical terms, they have been instantly and inexplicably absorbed into a black hole with no evident means of rescue. But things change after Lucy prays for a miracle of escape: "Aslan, Aslan, if ever you loved us at all, send us help now" (186).

Help does arrive, in the form of a great bird, an albatross, who whispers encouragement to Lucy "in a voice, she felt sure, was Aslan's." Like the "huge white birds" seen later, the albatross is evidently a beast of good omen. It is yet another godly animal, a trustworthy guide who enables the adventurers to find their way back to reality:

> At first it looked like a cross, then it looked like an aeroplane, then it looked like a kite, and at last with a whirring of wings it was right overhead and was an albatross. It circled three times round the mast and then perched for an instant on the crest of the gilded dragon at the prow. It called out in a strong sweet voice what seemed to be words though no one understood them. After that it spread its wings, rose, and began to fly slowly ahead, bearing a little to starboard. Drinian steered after it not doubting that it offered good guidance. (187)

---

defining presence in this East-running tale "about a journey toward the rising Sun," as Michael Ward argues in *Planet Narnia,* 108–15.

I think it likely that Lewis, in portraying this bird that at first "looked like a cross," would have been recalling and drawing upon Samuel Taylor Coleridge's classic poem *The Rime of the Ancient Mariner*. Coleridge's protagonist tells of how once through fog during his voyage there "did cross an Albatross," perceived by everyone on board as another "bird of good omen" and welcomed "As if it had been a Christian soul." By thoughtlessly killing this Albatross, the Mariner fatally violates his inherent membership in God's community of all creation, thereby bringing devastation upon himself and his fellow crew members. Yet the familiar, ecologically informed motto of Coleridge's poem is likewise an apt summation of Lewis's outlook as sustained throughout the Chronicles:

> He prayeth well, who loveth well
> Both man and bird and beast.
> He prayeth best, who loveth best
> All things both great and small;
> For the dear God who loveth us,
> He made and loveth all.[2]

By contrast with *The Dawn Treader*, the other world beyond Narnia that dominates the action of *The Silver Chair* is actually an Underworld, situated partly beneath the Narnian kingdom and partly beneath the wild waste land of giants to the north. And what most vividly in this tale stirs our recognition of the common beauty and goodness of God's creation is the contrast Lewis develops between the "sunlit lands" (*SC*, 140) of brightness above, whether Narnian or Earthly, as opposed to the Underland's dark realm of "strange beasts" and cheerless Earthmen. The sheer giftedness of life, for all of us "Overworlders" privileged to inhabit from birth to death our own planet's atmosphere of variegated radiance, wind, and sweet greenery, is easy to take for granted. But it's in fact a rare, divine blessing that Lewis's storytelling helps us take to heart. For the sunlit, fertile surface of the Narnian kingdom reminds us of Earth, far more than of those Hades-like caverns below Narnia's surface.

The Silver Chair opens in England, before the setting moves briefly with its protagonists into the heights of Aslan's country. They take a precipitous dive into Narnia and are led from there

2. Coleridge, *Rime of the Ancient Mariner*, in *Complete Poetical Works of Samuel Taylor Coleridge*, 189, 209.

first to the wild northlands inhabited by giants—then to the caverns, seas, and underworld city of the Dark Realm. The story's plot centers on a mission to rescue Prince Rilian, son of Caspian and rightful heir to the Narnian throne, from the evil clutches of a Green Witch who resembles the Jadis (White Witch) character of earlier tales. To achieve this restoration, Aslan calls on Eustace Scrubb and his schoolmate, Jill Pole, to find Rilian, and eventually to release him from his bondage in Underland. Jill and Eustace receive from the Great Lion four enigmatic signs that should presumably guide their pursuit.

As a literary scholar well versed in Greco-Roman writing, Lewis certainly appreciated the mythic overtones of this venture into the Underworld. Critic Peter Schakel points out that "the journey to the Dark Realm is reminiscent of the traditional trip to the underworld in classical literature, usually the greatest test of the hero's character."[3] For Eustace and Jill the journeying below is also, and perhaps supremely, a test of faith. For while Aslan had provided them with signs to follow toward a proper end to the quest, their way forward often remains shrouded in darkness and ambiguity. To interpret the signs successfully, they need plenty of discernment, persistence, and trust in Aslan's love and faithfulness.

By the time Eustace and Jill locate Rilian, in a remote subterranean cavern where he is shackled in a "curious silver chair" (162), the question of how to interpret the evidence of things seen and heard becomes particularly problematic. To begin with, the identity of the young man bound before them is far from clear. Who is this character, represented to them earlier as a rather ominous black knight, an unspeaking companion of the Queen of Underland? Is he actually the lost prince, veiled under a spell of the queen's enchantment? How, in any case, should they respond to his contradictory supplications? On the one hand, he warns them to ignore all subsequent pleas to loosen his bonds, since "when the fit is upon me" he will implore them to do that even though it is only "while I am bound" that "you are safe" (162). On the other hand, he insists only a little later that they must indeed "Quick! Cut these

3. Schakel, *Way into Narnia*, 76.

cords" because "at this hour" alone he is in his "right mind" even though he is enchanted "all the rest of the day" (164).

How, then, should they decide what, if anything, they should do? It is only because Rilian invokes the Great One's name, charging them at last "by the great Lion, by Aslan himself," that they rightly opt to set him free. And it is only "in the name of Aslan" that they can dare to proceed with that action (166, 168). So now, more than a decade after Rilian was lost in the woods and alienated from his true being, having suffered the Evil Queen's bewitchment of him and slaying of his mother, he finds instantly liberated and able to "remember my true self" (169).

The story's nonhuman creatures from Narnia contribute much toward this favorable outcome. Glimfeather, for example, the white bird who convenes a whole "Parliament of Owls," serves as a valued early ally to the children, transporting them in flight and advising them about several complications entailed in this mission. And at the story's climactic moment it's a gloomy but sage Marsh-wiggle creature from Narnia named Puddleglum who allows Jill and Eustace to cut through their indecision about how to act in the face of Rilian's pleas. Puddleglum points out that whatever may result from their actions, they have been told by Aslan exactly "what to do"—that is, they are to follow the signs they've been given, including the fourth sign revealing the prince to be the first person asking them "to do something in my name" (25). Faith and fidelity define the right way forward.

It is Puddleglum, too, who succeeds in banishing the deceitful spells turned upon all of them. In casting those spells the Evil Queen had insisted that "There never was any world but mine," that that "other world" of a Narnian Overland is simply a dream, never real at all. In much the same way, as critic Alister McGrath calls to mind, most of those who inhabit Lewis's Underworld, like those once lodged in Plato's allegory of the cave, "believe there is no other reality than the one they've come to know."[4] And for Lewis even the sunlit world above that *we* know represents, from

4. McGrath, *C. S. Lewis*, 301.

the standpoint of both Platonic and New Testament understanding, only the "bright shadow," or copy, of ultimate reality.[5]

Thus refuting the queen's nihilistic claim that neither Narnia nor any material Overworld exists at all, Puddleglum testifies with poetic fervor that "I know I was there once. I've seen the sky full of stars. I've seen the sun coming up out of the sea of a morning and sinking behind the mountains at night. And I've seen him up in the midday sky when I couldn't look at him for brightness" (176–77).

A comparable brightness suffuses Lewis's account of the tale's conclusion. Aslan then appears before the children as "the Lion himself, so bright and real and strong that everything else began at once to look pale and shadowy compared with him." And when Aslan blows the children home, they find themselves "standing in a great brightness of mid-summer sunshine, on smooth turf, among mighty trees, and beside a fair, fresh stream" (236–37).

"The greatest poverty," poet Wallace Stevens once wrote, is arguably "not to live / In a physical world."[6] Testimonies like those attributed to Puddleglum in *The Silver Chair* confirm that C. S. Lewis, too, appreciated the richness of experience in such a world. It is the sensory experience of living in just such a physical world that Prince Rilian likewise shows himself desperate to recover as he pleads to be rescued from his lifeless pit of despair:

> "Oh, have mercy. Let me out, let me go back. Let me feel the wind and see the sky . . . There used to be a little pool. When you looked down into it you could see all the trees growing upside-down in the water, all green, and below them, deep, very deep, the blue sky." (163–64)

The themes of baleful ambiguity and the unreliability of appearances woven into Lewis's portrayal of Rilian's speech from the chair are likewise reflected in the portrayal of the Evil Queen, otherwise called the Lady of the Green Kirtle. Before her demise she transforms herself into the guise of a "great serpent" that is "green as poison" (183). The vernal color imagery displayed in

5. McGrath, *C. S. Lewis*, 176–177.

6. "Esthetique du Mal," in *Poems by Wallace Stevens*, 124.

these references bears a penetrating irony. Ordinarily, of course, we expect a green hue to signify hope, freshness, biotic fertility and renewal. But in her deceitful bearing this Green Queen rules instead over a "black pit of a kingdom" (182). It is fitting, too, that she transforms herself into a serpent. As such she personifies in her death throes something of an anti-Eve, a mother not of life but of death, and one who promotes the antithesis of Eden. For adult readers, there is a further touch of irony verging on sarcasm in the author's mention of how the children's hyper-progressive school in England is so dismissive of religious values and tradition that "'people at Experiment House haven't heard of Adam and Eve'" (42).

Although Narnia's welfare and future governance are key concerns in *The Horse and His Boy*, most of this story's action unfolds elsewhere—in the lands of Calormen and Archenland to the south of Narnia. The book's setting in time reflects an earlier period than that portrayed in *The Silver Chair*. At this phase of the Chronicles, following from the closing events of *LWW*, Peter Pevensie holds sway as High King of Narnia. But *The Horse and His Boy* resembles *The Silver Chair* insofar as it is another tale about finding and restoring to proper rule a land's lost monarch—in this last case, the monarch of Archenland—whose true identity had long been unrecognized.

For the princely protagonist of *HB*, eventually revealed to Archlanders under the name of "Cor" (twin brother of "Corin"), that identity had long remained obscure even to the boy himself, who had been raised as "Shasta" and led to believe he was just the son or slave of an impoverished Calormene fisherman. Much of the plot addresses the complications of Shasta's arduous journey north to Narnia, through Archenland and desert wasteland, from his adoptive home in Calormen. It's an adventure he undertakes with a Narnian horse, Bree, and in the company of a girl, Aravis, who is likewise fleeing from Calormen with her Narnian horse, Hwin. Along the way this party briefly meets up with King Edmund and Queen Susan. In Anvard, the Archenland capital, warriors from Narnia help to defeat the Calormenes, who had conspired to take over both Archenland and Narnia, its ally. At that point Archenland's King Lune confirms that his son Shasta, now known as Cor, should be recognized as heir to the throne.

Green themes do not figure as pervasively in *HB* as they do in some other chapters of the Chronicles. But it is already clear from Lewis's placement of the possessive pronoun in his title, *The Horse and His Boy*, how deftly he has begun to upend our usual sense of the relation between ourselves as humans and the animals we think to possess—and that we suppose to exist almost solely for the sake of serving our own needs and desires.

The force of this reversal is elaborated through the manner in which the two horses, Bree and Hwin, are portrayed throughout the story. These talking animals not only take charge of the journey's pacing and navigation, but also guide much of its decision-making. Neither do they hesitate to take issue with their human "masters," even at times overruling them. From the start, for example, Bree tells Shasta that "as I intend to do all the directing on this journey, you'll please keep your hands to yourself" (16). Yet both horses also maintain a heartfelt solicitude for those they bear on their backs. So when Aravis had earlier felt so consumed with despair she thought to kill herself, it is her mare who speaks up to forestall that action. Aravis tells of how Hwin had "rebuked me as a mother rebukes her daughter" (38).

Despite its fantasy context, such descriptions can enlarge our own capacity as readers to imagine how the world might look and feel from the standpoint of nonhuman, sentient beings quite different from ourselves. Consider, for example, how Bree urges Shasta to run away with him, with a reminder of the speed his transport can provide. He remarks with a touch of droll wit on how "you can't get very far on those two silly legs of yours (what absurd legs human have!) without being overtaken" (13).

Both horses are quite willing to assist their human companions in the quest for liberation shared by them all. But they refuse to regard such service as involuntary servitude. Bree insists he is no longer a slave. He, like Hwin, came originally "from the free North," and knows himself to be "a free Narnian," even if he had previously for "all these years . . . been a slave to humans, hiding my true nature and pretending to be dumb and witless like *their* horses" (14, 12). One wonders, though, whether at least some of the "dumb" animals from our world might likewise be heard protesting their current ill treatment as slaves to humanity, as mere property, if they, too, could speak. Particularly in our own day of industrialized agriculture, when the ill treatment and hidden mass slaughter of animals for consumption has become a way of life, it seems fair to ask ourselves whether our culture's prevailing use of brute creatures amounts to anything better than slavery.

In that regard, the tension between slavery and freedom emerges as an overarching theme of Lewis's tale in *HB*, pervading both human and other-than-human spheres of creaturely existence. Narnia, unlike Calormen (along with other territories described in *The Dawn Treader*), qualifies as an emphatically *free* country in more ways than one. Human slavery has been outlawed in this land where even the Horse, too, can declare himself "a free Narnian."

Such plenitude of freedom is threatening to the Calormene leaders, who believe they should not "think twice about punishing Narnia any more than about hanging an idle slave, or sending a worn-out horse to be made into dog's-meat." They are disdainful of "these little barbarian countries that call themselves *free* (which is as much as to say idle, disordered, and unprofitable)." So they insist that Narnia is a land that should not long remain "unsubdued" (112).

Yet Bree, in his paean to that land of his birth where "nearly all the animals talk," links Narnia's creaturely freedom still more broadly to a physical environment that bristles with life and beauty. He rhapsodizes on this landscape's free-flowing plenitude:

> The happy land of Narnia—Narnia of the heathery mountains and the thymy downs, Narnia of the many rivers, the plashing glens, the mossy caverns and the deep forests ringing with the hammers of the Dwarfs. Oh the sweet air of Narnia! An hour's life there is better than a thousand years in Calormen. (11)

In the light of Christian theology, freedom can ultimately mean that the Creator has granted scope for genuine agency to all creatures, not just to humans. The Creator God is no puppeteer. Much as humans have been granted their own full scope of decision-making, toward evil as well as good, so also creatures of the natural order retain an agency of their own. They are never subjected to an absolute, programmatic control from above. And Aslan, whose presence in the story often calls to mind the wildness and redemptive force of God-in-Christ, is of course the story's freest being of all.

Aslan's portrayal in *HB* is arresting, differing in certain ways from his rendering elsewhere in the Chronicles. His bearing here is more palpably animalistic, more awesome and enigmatic and seemingly predatory, than in other Narnia chapters. In true leonine fashion, this "huge tawny creature" at one point jabs with his paw at Aravis enough to wound her. Although we're to suppose retrospectively that in doing so he wounds only to save, he is unapologetic about the pain this intervention causes her. And like the God Moses encounters within a burning bush, he refuses to disclose his name. When Shasta asks "Who *are* you?" he simply repeats, three times, the word "Myself" (165). Shasta imagines that during one night of terror, several lions had been chasing him and other members of his party. But a Voice, a Thing with warm breath, finally discloses to him that there had been just one animal involved—"I was the lion"—and his identity, like that of Jesus walking beside disciples on the road to Emmaus, had defied recognition at the time.

Yet Aslan, we learn, had all the while supplied the subtle yet saving presence, the non-compulsive agency, behind several turning points in Shasta's story: "I was the lion who forced you to join with Aravis. . . . And I was the lion you do not remember who pushed the boat in which you lay, a child near death, so that it came to shore where a man sat, wakeful at midnight, to receive you" (164–65).

In sum, the Aslan portrayed in *The Horse and His Boy* is a more troubling, fearsome animal than that seen in other phases of the Chronicles. Yet as Shasta comes to understand, the light this leonine figure sheds on his life-experience is nothing short of revelatory. In fact "No one," Shasta concludes, "ever saw anything more terrible or beautiful" (166).

QUESTIONS FOR REFLECTION AND DISCUSSION

1. The conversion of heart that Eustace undergoes in *The Voyage of the Dawn Treader* is a key feature of that story. But while Pope Francis has called for an "ecological conversion" of humankind, Eustace's transformation seems to have been even more specifically tied to a "zoological conversion." He had, in other words, earlier scorned Reepicheep the mouse and most other forms of animate life. He showed even more distaste for animals than for fellow humans. Yet eventually, after he is himself changed into a dragon, his behavior toward Reepicheep, Aslan, and other nonhumans changes drastically. How, then, does Eustace's new engagement with animal life and experience figure in this tale as both a *means* and a *consequence* of moral-spiritual conversion?
2. In *The Voyage of the Dawn Treader* Ramandu points out that a star isn't *only* a "huge ball of flaming gas." Such a strictly materialistic labelling doesn't capture a star's essence. It only describes what such a body "is made of." What relevance do you think this distinction bears for our larger, Earth-based inquiry into the nature of Creation's inherent materiality?
3. We can too easily take for granted our common experience of living on a green, sunlit, beauteous planet graced with a plethora of life-forms. So how might our imaginative engagement with worlds like the Underworld of *The Silver Chair* enrich our sense of the sheer giftedness of God's Creation as experienced on this Earth?
4. As discussed in this chapter, the Aslan portrayed in *The Horse and His Boy* mostly comes across as a more troubling,

fearsome, and outwardly animalistic figure than we find in other stages of the Chronicles. What do you take to be the impact and significance of this portrayal, especially in relation to Lewis's own ecotheological outlook?

5. Even the title of *The Horse and His Boy* encourages us to reconsider our usual confidence that we are rightly the masters, rather than the working partners, of both domestic and wild animals. Perhaps, in most phases of history prior to 1900, the sense of collaboration with equine partners was enhanced by humanity's need to rely so thoroughly on horses for transportation, various forms of industry, and agriculture. Yet how might we, even today, recognize ways in which our welfare is tied to that of animate nonhumans—not only as companions and (in John Muir's phrasing) "fellow mortals," but also as partners whose services are essential to our survival?

CHAPTER 5

The Last Battle and an Ending Without End

The Last Battle, the fictive endpoint of the Chronicles of Narnia, also inspires us to envision the End of the World—including the terminus of *our* world. The story's lurid apocalyptic imagery dramatizes toward its close the "last" stage of everything and everyone within the material order of life. The sun dies. The stars fall. Darkness extinguishes all light. And the land of Narnia, together with all those who inhabit it, meets its demise.

Yet beyond this endpoint *LB* tells of yet another, final act to the spectacle, situated "further up and further in" than the expected fall to oblivion. We glimpse a sunlit consummation of being beyond all the shadowlands of existence as commonly perceived either in Old Narnia or on present-day Earth. Lewis points us here toward nothing less an evocation of eternity, beyond the time of Narnia's last battle and, in fact, beyond time itself.

Lewis's sketching of this visionary breakthrough is consonant, though, with the Bible's more literal and essential sense of "apocalypse"—as focused not on cataclysm, but on the unveiling of an ultimate reality. In *LB* this revelation highlights the decisive transformation, rather than annihilation, of materiality. The essence of Old Narnia is preserved yet radically transfigured within the new dispensation of Aslan's "deeper country." It's through a stable's open doorway in Old Narnia that creatures of all sorts and conditions pass into the beatitude of Aslan's New World. And even *LB*'s reminder of an impending Day of Judgment offers a satisfying confirmation of Truth's final triumph over all lies and deceptions, including the Big Lie that Shift, the story's pernicious ape, had so widely promulgated.

PRÉCIS OF THE ACTION

This final installment of the Chronicles begins ominously "in the last days of Narnia."

From the outset Shift, a domineering ape, treats the donkey Puzzle, who is his neighbor and supposed friend, as though Puzzle were his servant. After pressing Puzzle to retrieve something glimpsed in Caldron Pool below a waterfall, Shift persuades the donkey to wear the lion's skin recovered from the water. Shift exploits this development to claim that the donkey, crudely disguised, is actually the Great Lion Aslan. He claims that Aslan answers as well to the name of Tash, a bloodthirsty Calormene deity. By swaying others to believe in the false Aslan, Shift also conspires with leaders from Calormen—including Captain Rishda Takaan and Ginger, a talking cat—in their plot to conquer Narnia and Archenland for themselves.

The ape uses a small hilltop stable to stage his display of Puzzle as the false Aslan, and much of the subsequent action takes place on Stable Hill. Shift also begins laying waste to the forests of Lantern Waste in western Narnia, part of his joint campaign with Calormen to challenge and overthrow existing rule in Narnia.

Narnia's King Tirian is hard-pressed to counter the sinister plots of Shift and the Calormenes. After rashly killing two Calormenes seen to be tormenting a talking horse, Tirian even becomes Shift's prisoner for a time. But throughout his trials, and in the face of popular distrust sown by Shift's falsehoods, Tirian can at least count on the support of a faithful unicorn, Jewel, and a centaur, Roonwit. In desperation, the king calls out to Aslan for assistance. He pleads for Aslan to "come and save all Narnia." He prays, too, for assistance from children and friends of Narnia living beyond his realm.

Although Aslan himself doesn't show up at this stage of the story, Jill Pole and Eustace Scrubb soon arrive as collaborators from Earth, having been plucked from a railway car there, and proceed to free Tirian and help him to rescue Jewel from the stable. With the donkey Puzzle, if not with the Narnian Dwarfs, they achieve some success in dispelling Shift's lies. But they mourn to learn that, with the king out of sight, Roonwit the centaur had been killed, Narnia's army had suffered a decisive defeat, and Cair Paravel had been taken under the banner of Calormen's leader, the Tirsroc. King Tirian must sadly acknowledge that "Narnia is no more."

Tirian and his remnant of Narnian loyalists return to Stable Hill, intending there to expose the ape's great fraud but with little hope of their own survival. At the stable, Shift and his cohorts have been wily enough to collude with Ginger the cat and Rishda Tarkaanto toward the destruction of all Narnian creatures induced to enter there. Yet Shift and his associates fall victim to their own machinations. Having previously summoned Calormen's terrible but presumably phantom figure of Tash, otherwise identified to Narnians as "Tashlan," Shift and Rishda Tarkaan are shocked to find that Tash is real. The ape meets his own demise from Tash when King Tirian throws him through the stable's doorway.

At this point Tash remains a threat to the remnant of Narnian loyalists. But before he can harm them, they are relieved to see a phalanx of honored Narnian royals appearing before them. That party includes Lucy, Edmund, Peter, Jill, Eustace, Polly, and Digory.

As Tirian and the others look out the stable door, they find themselves gazing now upon blue sky and grassy country. It seems that, depending on one's perspective and disposition, views from or into this stable open in multiple dimensions onto new vistas. The golden lion, Aslan, then appears. In these latter days of Narnia a multitude of diverse creatures leave that country, passing on their way through the open doorway. Narnia's losing combatants in a final grim battle, fought at night, likewise pass through the stable door, as do shortly all the children and friends of Narnia. This is evidently a death door, with the imagery of movement through it conveying a clear but palatable sense of mortality for Lewis's juvenile audience. At the same time it presumably offers a portal to larger life.

Before meeting their own mortal terminus, those gathered with Tirian grieve to see the stars fall, darkness advancing, and the old world of Narnia coming to an end. But after bidding farewell to this and all other Shadowlands, they are drawn "further up and further in" to reach the eternal, heavenly domain of Aslan's country. Everything and everyone of the old Narnia that mattered are gathered into this sunlit land, a sort of new Narnia but one experienced as more real and vibrant than its predecessor. The Pevensie children learn from Aslan that they, their parents, and others had perished on Earth in a railway accident, so their true home now is no longer in England but in Aslan's country.

A FEW PIVOTAL LINES . . . WITH MUSINGS ON THEIR MEANING IN THE LIGHT OF GREEN FAITH

> He had a little house, built of wood and thatched with leaves, up in the fork of a great tree, and his name was Shift. (3)

This description bears a quiet irony, reminding us that Shift the ape is very much an arboreal creature, fully connected to trees though he will soon be instigating their mass destruction in Lantern Waste.

> "But you think of the good we could do!" said Shift. . . . "Probably he sent us the lion-skin on purpose, so that we could set things to right." (14)

The sinister force of Shift's language here, as he browbeats Puzzle, lies in his suggestion that the plots he has conceived can truly advance virtue and serve the common good. Shift claims, in fact, to marshal much the same power for good as is commonly attributed to the Great Lion. There's a subtle irony, too, in the way

Shift's pretense to "set things to right" echoes Mr. Beaver's assurance in *LWW* that Aslan when he comes will "put all things to right."

> "They had not seen him, but they said it was certain he was in the woods." (17)

As King Tirian rightly suggests here, those faithful to Aslan can often begin to discern his presence in Narnia even when they have yet to see or hear him. The line recalls, too, that when he does return he is apt to dwell alone in the land's woodlands, rather than anywhere else.

> "Is it not said in all the old stories that He is not a tame lion?" (20)

Jewel makes this remark, which King Tirian then confirms. From *LWW* all the way to *LB*, various characters underscore the point that Aslan cannot be considered a *tame* lion. Along the way, though, the refrain takes on further shades of meaning. At base, this statement affirms Aslan's self-possessed freedom, his unfettered and godlike wildness beyond any control or compulsion. But particularly in this last installment of the Chronicles, it also suggests his radical unpredictability—a trait the Narnians find problematic as they struggle to discern his will amid an array of illusory representations.

> "Woe for my brothers and sisters! Woe for the holy trees! The woods are laid waste." (20)

This poignant lament of a beech tree's Dryad underscores our cognizance that trees, even those from our own world that cannot speak in words, are truly living creatures. Their hidden capacities, for pain and otherwise, lie beyond our ken.

> "Could it be true? *Could* he be felling the holy trees and murdering the Dryads?" (24)

It's scarcely surprising that at least some Narnians should express doubt whether Aslan, a champion of Narnia's woodland creatures, could be ordering their ruin. Shift's claim that Aslan could indeed have done so is belied, after all, by the biblical principle that by their fruits true witnesses can be distinguished from false ones.

> "Would it not be better to be dead than to have this horrible fear that Aslan has come and is not like the Aslan we have believed in and longed for? It is as though the sun rose one day and were a black sun." (30)

King Tirian witnesses here to the intensity of his faith in Aslan, the lodestar of his existence. The closing allusion also calls to mind the centuries-old Christian tradition of linking Christ, the light of the world and "Son" of God, to the physical sun.

> "We'll be able, with the money you earn, to make Narnia a country worth living in. There'll be oranges and bananas pouring in—and roads and big cities and schools and offices . . . and kennels and prisons—Oh, everything." (37)

Shift's profit-based justification for selling off many of Narnia's sacred trees is odiously materialistic. It also reflects a utilitarian vision of life that refuses to reverence the integrity of creation.

> "Do you think it really is Aslan?" asked the King."
> "Oh yes, yes, said the rabbit. He came out of the stable last night. We all saw him." (45)

The devil is reputedly a master of disguises, and Shift shows demonic wiliness in the way he manipulates appearances to serve his own ends. So even Puzzle's rather crude, lionskin representation of the Great Lion can apparently persuade at least some witnesses for a while. Because appearances can indeed be deceiving, the true Aslan is best discerned not just through sensory perception but through broader attention to his behavior, words, and values.

> "We're on our own now. No more Aslan, no more Kings, no more silly stories about other worlds." (83)

This disillusioned remark, voiced by some of the Dwarfs, suggests how the erosion of any discrete faith, especially one invested in things unseen, can readily devolve all the way to nihilism. Once these dwarfs cease believing in Aslan, they are inclined to reject as well the reality of worlds beyond their own, the re-creative power of imagination, and all prospect of transcendence. Real-life, Earthly counterparts of this linkage are not hard to find.

> "It seems then . . . that the stable seen from within and the stable seen from without are two different places."
>
> "Yes," said Queen Lucy. "In our world too, a stable once had something inside it that was bigger than our whole world." (161)

We are still apt to think of space and time, matter and energy, as discrete entities. That popular sense of things has a hold on us—despite the breakthroughs of modern science, including new notions about gravity, the curvature of space itself, and the space-time continuum.

Yet Lewis's account of the stable's relation to space and place challenges a simplistic view of such things. So depending on one's perspective, the stable's position in space can be perceived as two different places at once. And the contingency of its place in reality means that what's inside it can indeed be, paradoxically, larger than what's outside.

Plainly, too, Lewis's selection of a stable, as the focal point of Narnia's last days draws on Christianity's nativity narrative in St. Luke's Gospel, describing Jesus' birth in a manger. A rustic animal refuge in Bethlehem thus embodied an all-encompassing paradox, such that (as Lucy says) this "stable once had something inside it that was bigger than our whole world." That the presence of all heaven and earth could somehow be contained within Mary's womb is a marvel often recalled in Christian literary tradition.

"The whole country became bare . . . ."

> The difference between the old Narnia and the new Narnia was like that. The new one was a deeper country: every rock and flower and blade of grass looked as if it meant more. (196)

Statements like this suggest how the radically transformed paradise of the new Narnia nonetheless incorporates some physical features of the old Narnia. Much the same linkage could be supposed between our sense of a physical world, gleaned from our experience of living on Earth, and our intimations about the eternal realm of God. That realm, as Lewis portrays it, is not purely ethereal or abstract. The impressions of the heavenly realm he conveys in this passage are instead grounded in palpable facts of nature—rocks, flowers, blades of grass. These impressions are undeniably physical. Like Dante before him, Lewis supposed that no disembodied abstraction—but instead, unimaginable splendor—must characterize the ultimate fulfillment of God's new creation.

CONCLUDING THOUGHTS

For many readers, this concluding installment of the Chronicles comes as something of a disappointment. Previous books often brought to life the wondrous, enchanted character of that magical land called Narnia. But *The Last Battle* dwells instead on Narnia's lapse toward extinction. For the last Narnians, the battle in question ends in a devastating loss. There's a grim, unpleasant aura to much of the plot, aside from its closing sequences in the sunlit realm of Aslan's country. Much of this tale, steeped in death, dissolution, and the machinations of false prophets, can scarcely hold the charm both young and older readers had found in Lewis's wardrobe episodes. With Father Time marking Narnia's demise, *The Last Battle* is engulfed in the tragedy of mutability, death, and last things. As Michael Ward points out, the tale's elegiac mood corresponds to the way Lewis had elsewhere described the celestial figure of Saturn, embodiment of the "last planet / Old and ugly."[1]

1. From Lewis, "Planets," cited in Michael Ward's *Planet Narnia*, 193.

It is hard to know what to make of the strange, distressingly terse notice in Chapter 12 of *LB* that Susan Pevensie "is no longer a friend of Narnia." Given the dubious history of apocalyptic auguries, one could also question the story's use of end-time imagery from biblical texts such as the book of Revelation. And despite the increased sensitivity to racial-ethnic matters we rightly expect these days, well after the book's appearance in 1956, even Lewis's admirers must find it troubling to encounter signs of a cultural bias verging on racism in the evident contrast this author draws in *LB* and *The Horse and Its Boy* between the darker, presumably dissolute Calormenes and his favored, fairer-skinned Narnian characters.

Yet *The Last Battle* is well worth reading, I believe, for several reasons. For one thing, it reminds us unmistakably that everything we've come to know and love in the Shadowlands of mortal existence—whether played out on Earth or in Narnia—must finally come to an end. That's a sad lesson but one even juvenile readers need to start absorbing from an early age. As Jill remarks, she had hoped Narnia "might go on forever. I knew *our* world couldn't. I did think Narnia might" (182). *Every* particular belonging to what we call "the creation" counts as ephemeral, as merely transient in the long run. Of course at some point the text of Lewis's Chronicles, too, has to end—though it offers at least a shadow of God's endless Great Story "which no one on Earth has read" (211).

Beyond this elegiac feature, the work's biblically founded insistence on the power of false prophets and prophecies also rings true in the modern world. Who after all could forget, with this story's publication coming roughly a decade after the end of World War II, the ways in which widespread German credence in Hitler's big lie had convulsed and nearly destroyed the whole of global civilization? More recently, the Big Lie in other guises continues to spread disbelief in the reality of climate change while eroding the very foundations of democracy and the rule of law within the United States.

Shift's big lie includes the dream of turning Narnia into an amply funded, materialistic paradise. Such a transformation, even if achievable, would build no paradise. For to make "Narnia a country worth living in," Shift insists, would mean introducing lots of "roads and big cities and schools and offices and whips and muzzles and saddles and cages and kennels and prisons—Oh, everything." Everything, that is, by way of civilization's conventional and often restrictive artifacts. While preserving nothing of the pastoral land's beauty, love, communal interchange, spirituality, or natural fecundity.

Lewis was quite cognizant of the formative, potentially inspiring capacity of language. In scriptural terms the original source of creation itself is commonly attributed to God's spoken word. Christians have long revered the words of Jesus and the prophets as touchstones of truth and signs of the new creation.

In defiance of that truth, Shift deceitfully claims to speak with the authority of Aslan himself. He is the consummate devil and trickster, the parodic antithesis of God's truth. As such, he personifies the long-standing cultural tradition of identifying the devil with God's ape, *diabolus simia Dei*. Shift, like the devil himself, apes—but in the process also perverts—the ways of God. Shift claims to "set things to right" as though he had both the power and the benign will to do so. As the ape of God, the great deceiver constantly plays the role of "one that faines to imitate him though in contrary ways," in the words of seventeenth-century preacher John Gaule.[2] So the corrupting influence Shift's testimony has on trusting Narnians, hastening in turn the deformation of the natural order in that land, is especially offensive.

Two other features of Lewis's artistry in *The Last Battle* I also take to be germane to a theologically informed vision of care for creation. One of these relates to how Narnia's enemies have been laying waste to its forests. The report of that desecration, elaborated in chapter 2, has far-reaching implications for the story as a whole. The other feature I want to explore concerns the story's shift at the close toward radically transfigured states of being in Aslan's country, a sunlit and timeless realm distinct from anything

2. Cited by Stuart Clark in chapter 6, "The Devil, God's Ape," of Clark's *Thinking with Demons*, 82.

experienced in the Shadowlands of old Narnia or present-day Earth. Lewis's portrayal of this supernal realm clearly mirrors biblical expectations of a "new heaven and a new earth" (Rev 21:1; cf. Isa 65:17). It also stirs us toward a fresh consideration of how such a "new earth"—or, for that matter, a "new Narnia"—might relate to the material worlds they seem to displace.

Significantly, the first sign of Narnia's vulnerability and descent toward dissolution is that scene of massive deforestation pictured in chapter 2. It's a scene marked by the wailing of talking trees that are under attack. They are portrayed as sentient beings. The nymph of a beech tree cries her pain as the woods around her are ravaged: "Woe for my brothers and sisters! Woe for the holy trees." It is distressing to find Shift and his Calormene allies becoming unscrupulous despoilers of this enchanted environment. Shift initiates this incursion, though Calormen contributes laborers to the cause and soon exploits Shift to serve its own agenda. But why do Narnia's enemies choose in the first place to launch their aggressive campaign here, in the country's outlying woodlands? Why not *begin* by attacking the kingdom's capitol city, the castle of Cair Paravel, even though that site will eventually be taken by the Calormenes?

One explanation for the forest incursion is strictly monetary. Shift expects the sale of all those fallen trees, lashed together into rafts and sent down river to Calormen to yield a handsome profit there. But I believe there is a purpose larger than utilitarian gain behind this "murder of the Trees" (27). Because it strikes at the very soul of Narnia's identity and the spiritual source of its enchantment, the desecration of these holy trees is clearly meant to be dispiriting—not only for forest creatures, but for all who inhabit the land. Killing the Wood-Nymphs assaults the faith other Narnians, too, had long invested in the land's spirit-filled life, beauty, and sustaining virtue.

That is especially true given Narnia's portrayal in *LB* as a largely wild, agrarian country with few settlements. So the scale and character of this logging project anticipates the violation of agrarianism seen in the industrialized forms of agribusiness prevalent in our own day.[3] When Aslan first returns to Narnia the chief locus of his presence is not the castle of Cair Paravel, after all, but the presumption that he is "in the woods." And the Calormen assault on nature goes beyond tree killing. It includes as well cruelty toward animals. The Calormenes whip and drive mercilessly both the dumb brutes familiar in their own land and the talking horses they had enslaved from Narnia.

Like many clear-cut landscapes that are a sorry sight in our own world, the deformations wrought by intensive logging in Narnia resemble an open and ugly wound:

> Right through the middle of that ancient forest—that forest where the trees of gold and of silver had once grown and where a child from our world had once planted the Tree of Protection—a broad land had already been opened. It was a hideous lane like a raw gash in the land, full of muddy ruts where felled trees had been dragged down to the river. (26)

Chapter 14, titled "Night Falls on Narnia," describes the extinction of life in the country that had been the primary setting for all seven books in the Chronicles. The sun dies, all the stars (in "showers of glittering people") fall from the sky, and Time itself runs its full course to The End. Old Narnia is gone for good.

In the story's last two chapters, this elegiac strain gives way to a decidedly visionary finale focused on last things—that is, on Lewis's attempt to reimagine biblical "eschatology." The setting shifts from dying shadowlands to a glorious, sunlit land meant to signify a new engagement with ultimate reality—a timeless state that recalls traditional literary accounts of glimpsing the beatific vision. It's a land whose abundant fruits taste inexpressibly sweeter and better than any known in the Shadowlands. This closing sequence evidently draws on biblical prophecies about God's shaping

3. The unfortunate subversion of authentic agrarianism by industrialized agribusiness in today's mass culture is a pervasive theme in Wendell Berry's writing. And that theme's relevance to C. S. Lewis's outlook, as expressed in the Chronicles and elsewhere, is effectively elaborated by Matthew Dickerson and David O'Hara in *Narnia and the Fields of Arbol*, 123–29.

of "a new heaven and a new Earth" at the end of time, as well as on Plato's famous allegory of the cave in *The Republic*.

The stable's open doorway serves as the portal to this "great sunlight." It's a physically defined entryway that calls to mind Gospel allusions to the narrow gate through which many strive to enter the kingdom of God (Luke 13:24). And through *this* gate creatures of all sorts and conditions pass into the beatitude of Aslan's "deeper country." Some are visible saints. Some, like the Emeth character from Calormen, are formerly pagan seekers whom Aslan welcomes now as his Beloved Child. Others are Dwarfs, Satyrs, dragons, great lizards, dogs together with other animals familiar to us Earthlings, or odd unearthly beasts. King Tirian and the former monarchs of Narnia and Archenland are gathered there. Puzzle, the wayward donkey, appears there, too, but is transformed to bear a glowing coat and gentle face. Roonwit the centaur is there. Jewel the unicorn is there. So are Reepicheep the mouse, Farsight the eagle, and Tumnus the Faun. In fact, "everyone you had ever heard of (if you knew the history of these countries) is there" (205).

Predictably, the great Lion Aslan stands in grandeur amid it all. Emeth sees him as "more terrible than the Flaming Mountains of Languor, with a beauty that surpassed all that is in the world even as the rose in bloom surpasses the dust of the desert" (188). Toward the story's close he appears a figure of boundless vitality, "leaping down from cliff to cliff like a living cataract of power and beauty" (209).

The "deeper country" of timeless beatitude envisioned throughout this sequence looks to be, on the one hand, quite another world from the time and space of Narnia previously represented in the Chronicles. Yet its ties to the natural features of old Narnia reflect, on the other hand, a clear continuity.

Paradoxically, then, the "new Earth"—or in this case new Narnia—represented in Lewis's visionary conclusion reveals at once *difference from* and *connection with* the old Narnia. The visionary Narnia represents not an altogether *new* locus and spirit, so much as a *re*-newed condition of life. That's how we might best interpret the divine promise, in Revelation 21:5, to make "all things new." Such renewal suggests that anyone encountering its supreme reality there might well say with Jewel the unicorn, "I have come home at last! This is my real country! I belong here" (196).

Lewis dramatizes the new Narnia's relatedness to old Narnia by drawing on classic principles of Platonic thought. Digory points out that the Narnia its proponents once knew and loved, which had a distinct beginning and end, "was only a shadow or a copy of the real Narnia . . . just as our own world, England and all, is only a shadow or copy of something in Aslan's real world." Digory finds it consoling to recognize how "All of the old Narnia that mattered, all the dear creatures, have been drawn into the real Narnia through the Door." He remarks, too, on how this understanding of the new Narnia has very old roots, insofar as "It's all in Plato, all in Plato: bless me, what *do* they teach them at these schools!" (195).

The new world of Narnia, or of our own Earth, is best imagined, therefore, as a radical intensification and transformation of those material worlds we had already experienced. The oft-reiterated title of chapter 15, "Further up and Further In," says it all.

From the standpoint of creation theology, it is especially noteworthy that Lewis portrays the country of new Narnia as an intensely material and nature-encompassed realm. It is not merely a state of spiritualized, mental abstraction. It is not the sort of heaven which, as Matthew Dickerson and David O'Hara observe, is purely "ethereal," imagined to be "a place of disembodied spirits hovering on clouds (and playing harps)."[4]

Admittedly, the transformed materiality in question cannot be equated with our current notions or experience of material substances—just as the body of the resurrected Christ must be distinguished from the body with which he previously walked the Earth. But Lewis portrays the new, *supremely* real Narnia as a wide land abounding in real mountains, waters, skies, animals, orchards, grass, and flowers.

Like Narnia, the Earth as we know it is indeed passing away. That much is certain. But we should not therefore suppose that expectations of a future heaven permit us to become indifferent to

4. Dickerson and O'Hara, *Narnia and the Fields of Arbol*, 115.

this planet's health. I like to recall how one version of the Gospel story about Jesus' miraculous feeding of a large crowd with barley loaves and two fish concludes with Jesus exhorting his disciples to "Gather up the fragments left over, so that nothing may be lost" (John 6:12). I likewise take it as axiomatic that, within God's fullest dispensation, nothing is ultimately lost. Despite the countless deaths and diminishments to which all creaturely life is subject, that principle tells me that whatever might "follow" the end of all time and space in our current dispensation must have something essential to do with the material reality of that Creation as already known and reverenced.

This point is most forcefully conveyed, once again, through one of Professor Digory's statements. As he explains to the Pevensie children, the new Narnia's linkage to old Narnia amounts to an intensification rather than a negation of material reality: "The new one was a deeper country: every rock and flower and blade of grass looked as if it meant more. I can't describe it any better than that: if you ever get there you will know what I mean."

For Lewis, this notion of a sanctified materiality was grounded, above all, in Christianity's doctrine of the incarnation. That teaching played a key role in his personal conversion story, as can be gleaned from his memoir *Surprised by Joy*. It undergirds much of his writing, too, as evidenced in works such as *Mere Christianity* and, still more pointedly, in *The Screwtape Letters*. He never ceased to marvel at how that extraordinary incursion into history, when the eternal God took creaturely flesh in Jesus of Nazareth, had bridged the chasm between Creator and creation. And in the Chronicles he was inspired to imagine how the wild, altogether creaturely yet transcendent figure of Aslan could freshly embody that great mystery.

In recent years theologians have reflected further on the ways in which God's taking flesh as a flesh-and-blood temporal creature, described now as "deep incarnation," has expansive implications not just for humankind but for the whole of God's creation. For at least some Christians, the potential significance of the incarnation is now understood to be nothing short of cosmic. But Lewis, in his portrayal of Aslan, had arguably anticipated these developments several decades ago. Lucy's remark toward the close of *The Last Battle* captures this essence of deep incarnation, for "In our world, too, a stable once had something inside it that was bigger than our whole world." Something, and indeed Someone.

QUESTIONS FOR REFLECTION AND DISCUSSION

1. The often hidden life and vitality of trees is celebrated throughout the Chronicles. But *LB*, more than any other segment, dramatizes the evil of violating a world's community of life through massive deforestation pursued for monetary gain. Such violations likewise occur every day in our own day as great forests—including the Amazon's tropical rainforests and Northern Boreal woodlands—continue to be ravaged with clear cutting by corporate greed and consumer demands. These incursions clearly present a major obstacle to our hope of reducing the ills of climate change across the globe. Why, then, have the world's many citizens and groups who condemn this denuding of the land failed to stop it? What, if anything, might help to secure the protection of these great preserves?
2. Throughout much of *LB*'s narrative, the ape and false prophet known as Shift shows considerable cunning in launching his campaign of deceit in Narnia. Mixing lies and theatrical misrepresentations with half-truths, he succeeds for a time in persuading Narnians to deny even the best evidence available through their own sense experience. Many are led to deny even their faith in the goodness and godliness of Aslan. How might this fictional instance inform our understanding of how present-day denialism about climate change remains a potent impulse for many Americans, despite abundance evidence to the contrary?
3. For Lewis at the close of *LB*, as for Plato in antiquity, the forms of ultimate reality are shown to be more real than what

we take reality to be in the ordinary waking world. For Lewis these features of God's new creation are even shown to be, in some mysterious sense, more intensely *material* than what we now experience in Earthly space and time. If Lewis is right, what implications does this faith bear for our attitude toward Earthly creation?

4. In *LB* the tribulations suffered in the twilight of Old Narnia give way to the blissful consummation of a new creation in Aslan's country. It is fair to wonder, though: Is this vision of final things just a "pie in the sky" form of wishful thinking, as is often claimed? Does it mean, as some suggest, that we needn't worry about current environmental woes because God will ultimately step in to fix it all? How might you respond to these familiar arguments?

Conclusion

IN 1956, WHEN LEWIS'S *The Last Battle* first appeared, the modern environmental movement had yet to gain much footing or to stir public awareness. True, Albert Schweitzer's call to practice "reverence for life" had been heard by that time, as had Aldo Leopold's stirring case for conservation in *A Sand County Almanac*. The ecological ills of deforestation had long been apparent. And particularly after London's Great Smog of 1952, English city-dwellers were painfully cognizant of the misery from air pollution wrought by massive coal-burning. But in 1956 most of the world was decades away from concern about environmental issues such as acid rain, renewable energy, regenerative agriculture, or climate change.

Following from the preceding reflections on ecological overtones of the Chronicles it may therefore be worth asking again: What fresh insights might Lewis's exposition provide into the environmental crisis of our own day? In what respects, though, must we also critique this narrative's perspective on care for creation as dated, defective, or undeveloped?

Lewis's ecological vision does have its limitations. For example, the distinction he enforces throughout the Narnian tales between talking and "dumb" beasts is problematic in its implications for our own world. It may obscure rather than advance present-day inquiry into the furthest reach of animal intelligence, sentience, and capability.

Both within and beyond the Chronicles, Lewis's idealization of life in pre-industrial settings also has its limitations as we look to develop the most effective means of addressing the environmental challenges we face today in a world very different from that reflected in the feudal and monarchical social order of Narnia. Bio-technical expertise must be at least part of a contemporary response. It's true that Lewis, despite his penetrating critiques of "scientism," cannot fairly be regarded as hostile to science. Yet what's now demanded to sustain effective care for creation may require, among other things, our society's willingness to pursue more advanced understanding of intermediate technology, best energy practices, agronomy, and evolutionary science than Lewis could ever have been disposed to promote. Neither do all of his views, especially in later life, on evolutionary theory and development strike me as fully defensible today.

Much that's relevant to our world can still be gleaned from the Chronicles, though, such as the colorful array of beasts brought to life in its pages, including many species familiar to us Earthlings. That Narnia rightly belongs to its nonhuman inhabitants, no less than to its humans, is a conviction central to the Chronicles. The vibrancy, diversity, and agency of Narnia's animal life is a hallmark of the series. There can be little doubt about Lewis's lifelong appreciation of animals—his love of cats, dogs, and other animal companions, together with his disapproval of fox hunting and his vigorous objection to vivisection. He was reluctant to seek the demise even of the mice who shared space in his living quarters.[1]

At the time Lewis published *The Problem of Pain* (1940), he was still struggling to understand the nature and place of animals within the ordering of God's creation. In that work he rejected the possibility of attributing to bestial nature any sort of "soul" or "consciousness." He even doubted whether wild animals were honored by the same closeness to God he believed applicable to domestic beasts. "Man is to be understood only in his relation to God," he then insisted, and "The beasts are to be understood only in their relation to man and, through man, to God." He concluded that "The tame animal is therefore, in the deepest sense, the only 'natural' animal—the only one we see occupying the place it was

1. I comment further on these matters in "'Not a Tame Lion,'" 197–207.

made to occupy, and it is on the tame animal that we must base all our doctrine of beasts."[2]

From the first not everyone—not even all Christian admirers of Lewis—accepted this rather questionable argument. But I think Lewis deserves credit for his willingness over time to reconsider and eventually to revise his views on these matters. So by the time he published *The Lion, the Witch and the Wardrobe* in 1950, his imaginative inquiry had advanced to the point where his story's central character, the great lion Aslan, emerged as the apotheosis both of wildness *and* godliness.

As intimated in my Introduction, I consider it likely that the noted mystic and spiritual writer Evelyn Underhill played some role in this shift. On January 16, 1941, by way of responding to what Lewis had written in *The Problem of Pain*, Underhill sent him a largely appreciative letter in which she nonetheless challenged his claim that "the beasts are to be understood only in their relation to man and through man to God." As she dared to advise him, "I feel your concept of God would be improved by just a touch of wildness." Her surprisingly frank critique of Lewis's thinking is worth recalling insofar as his conception of Aslan would come to embody more than just a "touch" of wildness:

> "The tame animal is in the deepest sense the only natural animal." . . . This seems to me frankly an intolerable doctrine and a frightful exaggeration of what is involved in the primacy of man. Is the cow which we have turned into a milk machine or the hen we have turned into an egg machine really nearer the mind of God than its wild ancestor? . . . Your own example of the good-man, good-wife, and good-dog in the good homestead is a bit smug and utilitarian, don't you think, over against the wild beauty of God's creative action in the jungle and deep sea? And if we ever get a sideway glimpse of the animal-in-itself, the animal existing for God's glory and pleasure and lit by His light (and what a lovely experience that is!), we don't owe it to the Pekinese, the Persian cat or the canary, but to some wild free creature living in

2. Lewis, *Problem of Pain,* 138–39.

> completeness of adjustment to Nature a life that is utterly independent of man. . . . Of course I agree that animals too are involved in the Fall and await redemption and transfiguration. . . . Perhaps what it all comes to is this, that I feel your concept of God would be improved by just a touch of wildness.[3]

Underhill's remarks about the holiness of animal wildness may have struck a lasting chord in Lewis despite the skepticism he voiced about them when she first wrote to him. And he was certainly familiar enough with the Hebrew Bible to recall those poetic sequences in the book of Job extolling the untamed beauty, majesty, and freedom of animals such as the wild goat, hippopotamus, crocodile, eagle, bear, and lion. Untamed life is also celebrated in Psalm 104, which marvels at how "the young lions roar for their prey, seeking their food from God" (Ps 104:21). Moreover, the species of wild beast on which Lewis had centered his own reflection, toward the close of his chapter on "Animal Pain" in *The Problem of Pain*, happened to have been the lion.

Two other dimensions of Lewis's ecological vision, dramatized throughout the Narnian tales, strike me as especially noteworthy and instructive for us today. One of these features is the compelling but subsurface spring of theological meaning that suffuses the larger life of these tales. Reverence for the inherent holiness of creation is a hallmark of the Chronicles. Yet insofar as God's Creation warrants recognition—through the idiom showcased in *MN*—not for itself alone but as the love song of its Creator, it is never to be *worshipped* in a pantheistic light. For as Lewis observed in his *Reflections on the Psalms*, orthodox monotheism rather than pantheism can best heighten appreciation not only of nature's commonplace earthiness, but also of its potential for spiritual signification. "It is surely," he wrote, "because the natural objects are no longer taken to be themselves Divine that they can now be magnificent symbols of Divinity." So "by emptying Nature of divinity—or, let us say, of divinities—you may fill her with Deity, for she is now the bearer of messages" and holds sacramental

3. Underhill, *Letters of Evelyn Underhill*, 301–2.

meaning, whereas "there is a sense in which Nature-worship silences her."[4]

Although Lewis took humanity to be the crowning glory of God's creation, his worldview must finally be recognized as more theocentric than anthropocentric. Not only theocentric but also, given Aslan's crucial role in the fulfillment of salvation, decidedly Christocentric and incarnational. Lewis's characterization of the great lion, Aslan, presents us with a memorable, wonderfully arresting image of the nexus between Creator and creation, transcendence and fleshly immanence, the origins of life as well as its ultimate and redeemed destiny. And the force of that dramatization can be felt even by readers who happen either to resist or to feel removed from the teachings of orthodox Christianity.

A second noteworthy feature of Lewis's ecological vision in the Chronicles is the all-encompassing, cosmological context in which that vision is unfolded. The scope of creation envisioned in these stories is unspeakably vast, extending well beyond the country of Narnia. How many worlds might one imagine to exist beyond that of Narnia or, for that matter, beyond our own planet Earth? And which of these worlds might harbor intelligent but nonhuman creatures? If our God is indeed Lord of the entire universe, how might God's Word become known and enfleshed for those inhabiting planets other than our own?

Lewis had already begun to probe such questions in his novelistic space trilogy, as well as in the Chronicles of Narnia. Astronomers, too, now report the discovery of more "goldilocks" exoplanets or moons with life potential than was once thought possible. The vastness and variability of the universe that our Hubble and Webb telescopes have lately been disclosing is indeed awesome. It presents us with a cosmological splendor that Lewis's Narnian adventures cannot claim to mirror directly but may at least stir us to imagine more deeply, joyfully, and intensely.

4. Lewis, *Reflections on the Psalms*, 81–83.

Bibliography

Benz, Arnold. *Astrophysics and Creation: Perceiving the Universe through Science and Participation*. New York: Herder & Herder-Crossroad, 2016.

Berry, Wendell. "Christianity and the Survival of Creation." In *Sex, Economy, Freedom & Community*, 93–116. New York: Pantheon, 1993.

Carpenter, Humphrey. *The Inklings: C. S. Lewis, J. R. R. Tolkien, Charles Williams, and Their Friends*. Boston: Houghton Mifflin, 1979.

Carson, Rachel. *Silent Spring*. New York: Houghton Mifflin, 1962.

Clark, Stuart. *Thinking with Demons: The Idea of Witchcraft in Early Modern Europe*. Oxford: Oxford University Press, 1997.

Coleridge, Samuel Taylor. *The Rime of the Ancient Mariner*. In *The Complete Poetical Works of Samuel Taylor Coleridge*, vol. 1, edited by Ernest Hartley Coleridge, 186–209. Oxford: Clarendon, 1966.

Dickerson, Matthew, and David O'Hara. *Narnia and the Fields of Arbol: The Environmental Vision of C. S. Lewis*. Lexington: University Press of Kentucky, 2009.

Gatta, John. *Green Gospel: Foundations of Ecotheology*. New York: Church Publishing, 2024.

———. "'Not a Tame Lion': Animal Compassion and the Ecotheology of Human Imagination in Four Anglican Thinkers." In *Ecotheology and the Humanities: An Interdisciplinary Approach to Understanding the Divine and Nature*, edited by Melissa J. Brotton, 197–207. Lanham, MD: Rowman & Littlefield, 2016.

Jacobs, Alan. *The Narnian: The Life and Imagination of C. S. Lewis*. New York: HarperOne, 2005.

Johnston, Elizabeth. *Creation and the Cross: The Mercy of God for a Planet in Peril*. Maryknoll, NY: Orbis, 2018.

Lewis, C. S. *C. S. Lewis Essay Collection: Faith, Christianity and the Church*. Edited by Lesley Walsmley. London: Harper Collins, 2002.

———. *The Discarded Image: An Introduction to Medieval and Renaissance Literature*. Cambridge: Cambridge University Press, 1964.

———. *The Horse and His Boy*. New York: Scholastic-HarperCollins, 1954.

———. *The Last Battle*. New York: Scholastic-HarperCollins, 1956.

———. *The Lion, the Witch and the Wardrobe*. New York: Scholastic-HarperCollins,1950.

———. *The Magician's Nephew*. New York: Scholastic-HarperCollins, 1955,

———. *Prince Caspian*. New York: Scholastic-HarperCollins, 1951.

———. *The Problem of Pain*. New York: Macmillan, 1962.

———. *Reflections on the Psalms*. New York: Harcourt Brace, 1958.

———. *The Silver Chair*. New York: Scholastic-HarperCollins, 1953.

———. *Surprised by Joy: The Shape of My Early Life*. Orlando, FL: Harvest Harcourt, 1955.

———. *Till We Have Faces: A Myth Foretold*. Orlando, FL: Harvest Harcourt, 1956.

———. *The Voyage of the Dawn Treader*. New York: Scholastic-HarperCollins, 1952.

MacSwain, Robert. "Introduction." In *The Cambridge Companion to C. S. Lewis*, edited by Robert MacSwain and Michael Ward, 1–12. Cambridge and New York: Cambridge University Press, 2010.

MacSwain, Robert, and Michael Ward, eds. *The Cambridge Companion to C. S. Lewis*. Cambridge and New York: Cambridge University Press, 2010.

McGrath, Alister. *C. S. Lewis: A Life*. Carol Stream, IL: Tyndale, 2013.

McKibben, Bill. *The End of Nature*. 2nd ed. New York: Anchor-Doubleday, 1999.

Schakel, Peter J. *The Way into Narnia: A Readers' Guide*. Grand Rapids: Eerdmans, 2005.

Snyder, Gary. *The Gary Snyder Reader: Prose, Poetry, and Translations, 1952–1998*. Washington, DC: Counterpoint, 1999.

Stevens, Wallace. *Poems by Wallace Stevens*. Edited by Samuel French Morse. New York: Random House, 1959.

Tolkien, J. R. R. *The Tolkien Reader*. New York: Ballantine, 1966.

Underhill, Evelyn. *The Letters of Evelyn Underhill*. Edited by Charles Williams. Westminster, MD: Christian Classics, 1989.

Ward, Michael. *Planet Narnia: The Seven Heavens in the Imagination of C. S. Lewis*. Oxford: Oxford University Press, 2008.

Williams, Rowan. *The Lion's World: A Journey into the Heart of Narnia*. Oxford: Oxford University Press, 2012.

www.ingramcontent.com/pod-product-compliance
Lightning Source LLC
LaVergne TN
LVHW090529110826
845146LV00003B/1034
* 9 7 9 8 3 8 5 2 4 3 5 9 4 *